S0-ALK-893

FIC
SCHRAFT Schraft, Constance
                Instead of you

DATE DUE

OCT 6 '90	NOV 14 2010	
15 91	OCT 19 2012	
MR 13 '91		
AP 4'91		
OC 7'92		
FEB. 2 3 1998		
FEB. 1 2 1999		
JUL 0 2 1999		
AUG. 2 0 1999		

Gilpin County Public Library
Post Office Box 551
Black Hawk, Colorado 80422

DEMCO

Instead of you /
FIC SCHRAFT   203435

39204000021503

Schraft, Constance.
Gilpin County Public Library Colorado

instead of you

instead of you

constance schraft

TICKNOR & FIELDS

NEW YORK

1990

Copyright © 1990 by Constance Schraft

All rights reserved

For information about permission to reproduce selections
from this book, write to Permissions, Ticknor & Fields,
215 Park Avenue South, New York, New York 10003.

Library of Congress Cataloging-in-Publication Data

Schraft, Constance.
Instead of you / Constance Schraft.
p.   cm.
ISBN 0-89919-948-8
I. Title.
PS3569.C52846157   1990
813'.54 — dc20   90-32156
CIP

Printed in the United States of America

BVG 10 9 8 7 6 5 4 3 2 1

GILPIN COUNTY PUBLIC LIBRARY

C
SCHRAFT

For my family

For their support during the writing of this book, I wish to thank Betsy Berne, Andrea Chapin, Louisa Ermelino, and Barb Hey. I'm grateful to Yaddo for my visit there and to Fran Kiernan, who worked with me from the start. My deepest thanks go to my boys, Don and Willie.

instead of you

ONE

MY SECOND NIECE was named after Saratoga. We were at the racetrack the day she was born — my sister, Charlotte, her husband, Sam, and I. It was August. The three of us were sharing a cabin on a quiet lake north of town. Only Charlotte had wanted to come to the track, and only Charlotte was having any luck. She kept a record of her winnings on a cocktail napkin, which she also used to pat her forehead. After each race she jumped up and down until Sam finally grabbed her wrist and said, "What're you trying to do, have that baby right here?" She wasn't due for another month.

During the trifecta, she let a man in a straw bowler touch her belly for luck. A round of pink, frothy drinks arrived — on him, the waitress told us. "I shouldn't drink this," Charlotte said, but she took tiny sips until the glass was empty. Then she leaned toward me and whispered, "I've got something to tell you."

"Lou and I are going to take a look at the horses," she told Sam. She had a theory that the way to pick a horse was to examine its knees.

"What is it?" I said, smoothing the wrinkles from my dress as we stepped out of the grandstands, into the sunlight. But she said, "Come on," and started toward the paddocks. I was used to that. She'd been doing it since we were kids — promising to tell me something, then torturing me, making me wait.

But then, she stopped short. "Would you please just tell me?" I said.

She sank to her knees, her pale blue skirt mushrooming around her. "Get Sam," she said, the words trickling out like the last drops in a canteen.

On the way to the hospital, Sam said, "Couldn't you have been more careful? Couldn't you have tried, just this once?"

"Slow down a little, sweetheart," she said, bracing her hand against the dashboard.

Every doctor in town was at the track that afternoon. Sam and I stood on either side of Charlotte's bed. Between contractions, all she could say was "Don't stare!" When the anesthesiologist finally arrived, he gave her a shot of something and she stopped thrashing. She wanted to know which horse won the last race.

She was a year, three months, and ten days older than I. She claimed she taught me how to climb out of my crib. I could picture her rattling the bars, egging me on in baby sounds. In grade school, boys chased her home; she showed me her escape routes.

When the time came, she taught me how to kiss. "Close your eyes a little, tilt your head," she'd say, and I practiced until I got it right. Following her to college, I took the exact same courses. I figured that if my brain contained what hers did, I'd be like her.

But my strategy failed. At school we both dressed in fatigues and olive-drab T-shirts and stood in front of the cafeteria with leaflets advocating the boycott of grapes and iceberg lettuce and California wine, but I knew we didn't feel the same. When Charlotte addressed our campus chapter of the United Farm Workers, I wondered where she'd learned to speak that way. I wondered how she could care so much for people she'd never even met.

When she decided to join the Peace Corps and move to the Ivory Coast, I wasn't surprised. Since we'd been girls, her fortune cookies had predicted adventure, while mine began, "Beware." But after a lot of thinking, I decided I wasn't going with her. The Ivory Coast was unknown and far away. Besides, I was tired of following. It took too much out of me. You'd think the opposite. You'd think that walking in a path already cleared would require less than forging your own. But following Charlotte, I was fighting my own chemistry. I was always in battle.

I worried about telling her. I assumed she'd become as accustomed to having me beside her as I was to being there. Like losing an arm or losing an audience, my absence would come as a shock, I supposed.

But when I finally brought up the subject, Charlotte was startled. "Of course we can't go places together anymore," she said. "I have to do what I have to do, and you have to do what you have to do."

Instead of feeling relieved, I was anxious all over again. How would I know what to do if she didn't tell me?

Sam Asher was finishing his dissertation in macroeconomics when Charlotte met him. He wasn't her type; she'd always gone for big, burly guys. Sam was slender and handsome and impeccably neat. He'd recently cut his hair, and I'd never seen him once with a five o'clock shadow.

When he and Charlotte started going out, no one thought it would last. But soon we noticed that Charlotte was combing her hair more often, and when someone asked her a question at one of our farm workers' meetings, instead of being ready with an answer, she blushed and had to ask for the question to be repeated. Then she shook her head. "We can't go on hounding people," she said. Before, she'd never thought twice about hounding people for a good cause.

When he left school, Sam was going to take a job he'd been offered at an investment banking firm, but in the meantime he read poetry and smoked marijuana to collect his thoughts and he told Charlotte that if he didn't enjoy working in finance, he'd quit and become an auto mechanic instead. He cared for his MG as if it were a helpless child. On the road, though, it was a different story. Giving Charlotte and me a ride home the first Christmas they were together, he drove so fast that the arch in my right foot ached from braking.

On the way he asked what kind of cookies our mother was baking for the holidays. "Pfeffernüsse and Russian tea cakes," Charlotte said. "Butter cookies in shapes with colored frosting."

I thought he was just making conversation, but when we got home, Sam sat down at the kitchen table and admired each variety of cookie before devouring handfuls. "There won't be any left," I whispered uneasily to my mother.

"Your sister's going to marry that man," she prophesied.

"Charlotte?"

"I don't see any other sister."

When we went back into the kitchen, Charlotte was watching Sam. I recognized the softness around her eyes that appeared when she was speaking of an endangered species or the children of migrant farm workers.

"Someone should play a Christmas carol," my mother said. "Go on, Charl."

"Make Lou," Charlotte said. "She has a better touch."

"I do not."

"You do too," she said. "You've always had a lovely touch."

All evening her words resounded inside my head. I pictured soft hands with tapered fingernails on the piano keys. I pictured myself in a black velvet dress before an audience. If I could play well enough, I wouldn't have to speak.

A week before her graduation, Charlotte found out she was pregnant. "This is not what I expected of you, Charlotte Marie Post," my mother said.

It wasn't what anyone had expected. A friend of Charlotte's told her the name of a doctor who would safely take care of the problem. "What problem?" Charlotte asked.

My father could hardly look in her direction. "Once everyone gets over the shock, they'll be happy for me," Charlotte predicted.

"Look who's such a know-it-all," said my mother, but then she smiled.

That meant she was genuinely happy; she didn't hand out smiles freely. Either everyone was changing, or somewhere along the line, I'd gotten lost. Now that she was pregnant, Charlotte seemed to have forgotten about going to Africa. Each time Sam lifted Charlotte's shirt and kissed her belly, my mother smiled again. And Charlotte was right; my father soon came around.

After they were married, Sam and Charlotte found a two-bedroom apartment in New York City, with good light and a decent-sized kitchen. Until the baby was born, Charlotte took the bus across Seventy-second Street five days a week for French conversation classes. Afraid of losing her fluency, she insisted on speaking French whenever I came down from school to visit.

"We were going to live in Paris," I reminded her one day. "Remember? We used to practice writing love letters in French. *Tu es mon coeur.*"

Her eyes widened. She got up and disappeared down the hall.

When she didn't come back soon, I went looking for her. She was in the bathroom standing naked, sideways, in front of the full-length mirror. Her arms and legs and face had stayed the same, and her collarbone still protruded when she finally shrugged and looked away, but her breasts and stomach were inflated like balloons.

The spring after Annie was born, I graduated from college and moved to the city, where I didn't know a soul but Charlotte and Sam. Whenever I called, Charlotte would invite me over. The minute I arrived, though, she'd be out the door with her duffel bag, off to the gym. She was struggling to get back in shape.

Alone in their apartment, I wandered from room to room,

examining their things as if I were in a gift shop. In the park I watched the Hudson while Annie dozed in her carriage. When people stopped to admire her, I pretended she was mine. "Five months," I'd say. "She's big for her age." In the fall I began giving piano lessons to neighborhood kids and teaching theory at a nearby music school. Occasionally I went out on a date — nothing serious, just a friendly guy who lived above me, and now and then, I'd go to the movies with a woman I'd met at a concert. Gradually, the tempo of my life quickened and I hardly ever made it uptown to see Charlotte anymore.

I half regretted saying no all the time when she called; I missed her. But another part of me was glad. She'd never stopped expecting me to be there.

That spring, as lessons were winding down for the season, I happened to have a free night when Charlotte telephoned. I agreed to take care of Annie so that Charlotte and Sam could go to the ballet.

When I arrived, Charlotte was trying to get dressed and Annie was in the way, adorning herself and a funny-looking black-haired doll named Ernie with Charlotte's necklaces and perfume. "Make her disappear," Charlotte begged me, so I took Annie to the park.

Somehow we lost Ernie. "Either we forgot him in the sand-box, or he fell out of the stroller coming home," I told Charlotte.

"Don't worry, she's got a million dolls," Charlotte said. As she bent to kiss Annie good-bye, I saw that her dress was backless. She'd been lifting weights, and every move she made set off a wave of muscle beneath her skin.

"Where Ernie?" Annie asked when I was putting her to bed, but she was surrounded by a menagerie and didn't seem disturbed by his absence. A few hours later, though, she woke screaming and climbed out of her crib. She ransacked her toy chest and closet and tore through the apartment, searching beneath the couch and in the bathtub, where she'd once taken Ernie swimming. An hour later, she sobbed herself to sleep.

When Sam and Charlotte got home, I told them what had happened. "She's experiencing loss," Sam said.

"Oh, come on," said Charlotte. "She knows her dolls aren't real. She's lost things before. She had a nightmare, that's all, and we weren't here. She's still just a baby."

But the next time I came over, Annie wouldn't come near me. "She thinks I'm after her new Ernie," I told Charlotte.

"She forgot about that ages ago."

"Just watch. She's acting different with me."

"You still remember, so you assume she does. Kids forget. Everything distracts them." Charlotte sighed. "Frankly, right now I'm more concerned with getting her into a decent play group for the fall."

That summer, out of the blue, Charlotte and her family moved to the suburb where she and I had grown up and where our parents still lived. Charlotte hadn't told me she was even considering this. "We need a bigger place," was her explanation when I said she was crazy. "We're planning to have another baby."

I put my foot down and refused to help with the move, but Charlotte didn't seem to notice. She had my parents now. "I knew the city was no place to raise kids," my mother said.

In college, the off-campus house where Charlotte and I had lived held six of us plus an ever-changing array of boyfriends and pets. No one cared whose was whose; no one locked doors. The floorboards creaked, and when the animals ran through a room, scatter rugs slid after them.

Now Charlotte discarded her futon and bought a bedroom set. The three redwood Adirondack chairs that had been her living room furniture in the city were relegated to the backyard. Her new home came equipped with wall-to-wall carpeting, a burglar alarm, and central air conditioning. The pot holders said "Charlotte's Kitchen," and all the plates matched. There was an underlying organization to the contents of the cabinets and closets and drawers; even cereal boxes had a definite location.

Everything about the house was wrong. Everything about

Charlotte was wrong. When I blasted the Rolling Stones, as I was sunbathing in her new backyard, she shouted, "Turn that down!"

In that town up the river, the public schools were reliable, and everyone belonged to a church. By the time Sara was born a year later, Sam had been promoted to senior vice president and Charlotte had planted a serious garden. Her perennials were in full bloom — rows of irises, hollyhocks, Shasta daisies, and poppies. To get started, she'd bought flats of marigolds and impatiens, but in the future, she planned to grow her annuals from seed, and someday, she was going to convert the back porch into a greenhouse.

There were gardening books everywhere you looked, but Charlotte's inspiration came from the Impressionists. "Squint," she said to me when we were sitting on her terrace one afternoon in July. "Isn't it a Monet?"

Hearing that, I chortled and spilled my wine, and Charlotte hurried inside for a sponge and seltzer to remove the spot from my shirt. While she was gone, I took another look around, but I still couldn't see a painting. Instead, I remembered Charlotte drenched in sweat earlier that day, pulling up weeds even though she was seven months pregnant.

I looked at my watch that afternoon to see what train I could catch back to the city. How could Charlotte live out here, I wondered, with the same old sky we'd grown up under and a tree that cast the same shadow as the oak that had sheltered us and our checkerboard from the sun when we were girls?

By the time Charlotte finally waddled out the back door, I was on my feet. "You can't go yet," she said, refilling my glass with a wine that the *New York Times* had recommended, but I made her drive me to the station.

"I'm so glad you girls have stayed close," my mother often said. Well, we were, and we weren't. We could raise the hair on each other's necks; we knew how to draw blood. But practically every single one of my visits was followed by a phone call to clear up a misunderstanding, and never once did I get up to leave without Charlotte looking disappointed. "Do you really have to go so soon?"

I took terrible pleasure in leaving before she was ready to let me go. It was terrible pleasure because I didn't really want to go; I just wanted to see that Charlotte minded. But at the station, she'd wave good-bye and drive off, and in the end, I was the one left behind. Standing on the platform, I'd wonder if she'd been waiting all along for me to leave so she could get back to her garden and her family.

The summer Sara was born, I agreed to go to Saratoga with Charlotte and Sam, because Charlotte complained, "We hardly ever see each other anymore."

"Whose fault is that?" I'd asked. "Who moved?" It was typical. When she wanted company, I was expected to drop everything.

But what did I have to drop? Piano lessons weren't given during the summer, and the guy upstairs had moved to Atlanta. All I had to drop, really, was a copy of *War and Peace,* which I sometimes wished would drop of its own accord, from the fire escape of my apartment, while I was inside fixing iced tea. Everyone advised me to skip the war parts, but I felt I had to get them straight. I kept a map of nineteenth-century Europe beside me as I read.

After Sara was safely delivered, Sam and I left the hospital and drove back to the cabin we were renting. There was no moon that night. The trees whispered on both sides of the road, pines that sagged and slumped during the hot, still days, only coming to life in the dark.

"I don't know what I'd have done without you," Sam said.

"You'd have been fine."

"Isn't the human body amazing?"

"I thought she was going to die."

He nodded. "I know what you mean. I thought that the

first time. Like her body was going to split in half, right up the middle."

"I could see all the way inside her," I said.

"Amazing," he repeated.

"I wish I hadn't seen it."

But Sam had stopped listening. His second child had just been born. "I think there's a bottle of cheap champagne in the fridge," he said. "Sparkling something. Something the owner left. We can celebrate with that." He laughed softly, shaking his head. "Amazing," he said again.

"It's not so bad," Charlotte told me the next day, cranked up to a sitting position in her hospital bed. Sam had let slip that I'd been afraid. "And look what you get in the end," she added, handing me the tiny bundle.

two

AROUND THE CORNER from my apartment in the city was a municipal swimming pool. Housed in a dank brick building, it had seen better days. Only people who couldn't afford a membership at a health club would step foot in it. I'd been swimming there regularly for almost eight years.

Stenciled on the wall at the deep end was the warning AB-SOLUTELY NO DIVING. It hardly seemed necessary. Swimmers sat gingerly at the pool's edge while their feet and calves registered the frigid water. Only gradually, grimacing, did they slip in.

One winter evening while I was taking a rest after my first thirty-five laps, a man walked in with hair long enough to require a bathing cap — a rare sight those days. Dropping his towel on a bench, he fitted a white rubber cap over his head, and I could see his features clearly, dark eyes and a wide mouth.

As the man marched toward the deep end of the pool, the lifeguard, who ordinarily did no more than snap his fingers to the music on his Walkman, jumped down from his chair and lifted his whistle to his lips. "Don't try it, bud," he called.

The man smiled apologetically and dove flat, shaving the surface of the water. "Wise guy," hollered the guard, and he blew his whistle furiously.

The man swam the length of the pool. He had a strong kick, but he lifted his head too high when coming up for air. He wasted precious energy that way; he created resistance.

After my swim I often stopped at a café on Hudson Street where I'd gotten to know the waitress. If business was slow, she'd sit down at my table and chat. That night, she brought along a dish towel with the cappuccino I'd ordered so that I could dry my hair, which was hanging in straggly icicles. When the man from the pool came in a few minutes later, she said, "What you need, Lou, is a hat like his."

She spoke loud enough for him to hear, and he turned around. He'd changed from his bathing cap to a shearling-lined hat with ear flaps. "I'll have a double espresso," he told the waitress, coming over to my table. To me, he said, "My name's Richard Easton. I'll show you where you can buy a hat like this."

He sat down, took a pen from his pocket, and drew a map on a napkin, directing me to the store. He took the hat off and described its features, the same way a stewardess would demonstrate the emergency procedures on an airplane. As he talked, he sipped his espresso, and when he'd finished it, he put his hat back on and stood up.

I tried to imagine what Charlotte would do to prevent him from leaving. She wouldn't pull the newspaper out of her swim bag. She wouldn't thank him and avert her eyes. "That's a nice pen," I finally said. "Where'd you get that?"

Richard's eyes narrowed. He told me later that he prided himself on his ability to size people up accurately, in moments, and it was the last thing he'd expected me to say.

Richard was a screenwriter, working on his first feature-length movie. During my years in the city, most of the people I'd become friends with were trying to do things like be writers or painters or musicians, but he was the first I'd met who wasn't a wreck over it. As I got to know Richard, I decided that he was going to succeed simply because the thought that he might not never crossed his mind.

Richard was as unlike me as anyone I'd ever met. He didn't go around looking for confirmation from other people. He wasn't constantly trying to second-guess himself. He didn't think my flaws were worse or more numerous than anyone else's. And when he met Charlotte, he didn't fall for her. More than anything else, that made me love him.

By the time spring arrived, I was spending almost every night with Richard. In May, on my thirtieth birthday, he asked me to move in with him.

I already kept some things in his dresser drawers and closet, but what I needed always seemed to be at my place. When I went home for a book or a pair of earrings or a springform pan, I'd open all the windows to air out the musty smell that seemed to envelop the rooms the moment I left. I'd sit in the rocker and look around and feel content as I never had before. It seemed a shame that I'd never fully appreciated solitude until now, when I had so little of it.

On my birthday, Richard said, "Move everything over here. I don't want there to be any reason for you to ever leave."

But I resisted. I'd reached this point with another guy, but that hadn't stopped him from making a pass at Charlotte. Where would I have been if I'd given up my apartment the way he'd asked me to? Richard was different, I knew that, but he wasn't perfect. His answering machine messages were obnoxious, and he could ruin a movie, whispering loudly the whole time it was running, criticizing the lighting and the camera angles and the script. He didn't think teaching was enough and wasn't afraid to tell me so. "With your talent, you should be performing," he insisted. When I said I didn't want to, he'd sigh in a loud, melodramatic way.

But basically, things were going so well that when summer came around that year, even though I'd barely known Richard six months, I screwed up my courage and invited him to come along to my grandfather's annual Fourth of July party.

My mother's father was a patriot. For him, Independence Day was the only real holiday. Every July he invited the family up to his place, a rambling stone house on a lake in the Berkshires, and unless you were dead or dying, you made it up there. Once, so we wouldn't end up in the doghouse, Charlotte and I hitchhiked all the way from Spring Lake, New Jersey, where we were waitressing for the summer, arriving grimy and quarrelsome at dusk.

If his arthritis was acting up, my grandfather made his older sister, Clara, hang the red, white, and blue crepe paper streamers around the front door, but he much preferred to do it himself. He said that Aunt Clara, who favored masking tape over tacks, didn't fasten the streamers securely.

Aunt Clara defended herself, insisting that the old doorframe wasn't strong enough to withstand the treatment it received each July. When my grandfather hammered with all his might, humming "You're a Grand Old Flag," she clapped her hands to her ears.

Unlike her brother, Aunt Clara considered herself a citizen of the world. Her third husband, now dead, had been a retired airline pilot, and they'd flown all over on discounted airfares. Aunt Clara had had acupuncture in China and shiatsu in Japan. Though she was in her eighties, she claimed that, thanks to those treatments, she never suffered a moment's pain.

That his sister had permitted a Japanese person to touch her body infuriated my grandfather; he was unforgiving on the subject of the war. "Overcome your pride, Charles," Aunt Clara would counsel him. She thought the Japanese knew best how to eat, cure illness, and write poetry. In her opinion, Walt Whitman was full of hot air.

Aunt Clara had moved in with my grandfather after my grandmother, still a young woman, died of a stroke. My mother, their only child, had been away at college. Aunt Clara was between husbands at the time, and had no children of her own; besides, she felt responsible for her brother, who was accustomed to having everything done for him. The day she moved in, there were no lights in the kitchen, and when she asked what had happened, my grandfather told her that a fuse had blown three days before.

A year later, though, Aunt Clara moved out and got married again, this time to an old friend of her first husband. "I couldn't settle in," she confessed to my mother. "The middle of the night, Charles would be prowling around, making sure I hadn't moved anything. And the way he shouted — the local grocery refused to sell to him anymore because he was always haggling over prices. Ten miles we had to drive to a big new supermarket you could get lost in, and still I'd hear him bellowing at the butcher from halfway across the store."

But when Uncle John, her third and last husband, died, Aunt Clara moved back with my grandfather for good. She had no choice. It turned out that she had practically no savings and nowhere else to go. This time, she did the best she could. She tried to keep my grandfather from eating fried steak every night and sleeping without sheets. She tried to keep him from biting my mother's head off when the family came to visit. "Appreciate her, she's your golden child," Aunt Clara would say. What bothered my grandfather, what he reprimanded my mother for without ever coming out and saying it, was that she was not a son. The family name would die with him.

Going to the Berkshires that weekend, Richard insisted I drive his car in case he needed to photograph something along the road. He always fully expected to see something spectacular. He got a lot out of life, thinking that way.

Just over the Connecticut border, he shouted, "Hold it, stop!"

"What?" I veered off the highway.

"That tree —"

"What tree? Which one?"

He was already out of the car, adjusting the lens of his camera. "This is the shot of a lifetime," he said, though it looked like an ordinary oak to me.

"Pull over!" he hollered a little later.

"What now?" I came to a halt on the shoulder.

He dragged me out his side. "Hurry," he said, urging me through the ragweed and scraggly maples that bordered the highway.

"You're ravishing," he murmured when we reached an ugly little clearing littered with smashed beer cans and cellophane. His lips were like suction cups, emptying the air out of me, but I kept listening over his shoulder to the traffic.

Finally, I said, "Richard?"

"What?"

"How'd you know about this place?"

He held me away so he could see my face. "I've been on this road before." He gave me a little shake. "I'm thirty-seven years old," he said. "I'm not going to pretend I was born yesterday."

When we pulled into the driveway of my grandfather's house, Sam waved us to a spot beneath the weeping willow. He hugged me but acted cool with Richard. They'd met twice before. The first time, Richard took Charlotte, Sam, and me to a bar in his neighborhood, and there, our waiter got into a fist fight with someone at the next table. The more recent time was at Sam and Charlotte's. While Richard was playing tag with the girls, Sara fell on the flagstone terrace and had to get three stitches in her forehead. To Sam, Richard was synonymous with trouble.

"Charlotte and your mom ran out for a case of beer," Sam told me. "Your grandfather and Aunt Clara aren't speaking."

"Already?" Most mornings, they stayed out of each other's way. For the sake of his digestion, my grandfather didn't like to start arguing until after lunch.

When Richard and I went around back, my grandfather and Aunt Clara were sitting under trees at opposite ends of the lawn. Even though we were closer to Aunt Clara, I brought Richard over to meet my grandfather first. Otherwise, I'd have paid for my mistake all day.

"So this is the moviemaker," my grandfather said, neither getting up nor holding out his hand. He shook a newcomer's hand only after circling and sniffing him like a dog. I'd pre-pared Richard for that. I'd spent an awful lot of time explain-ing my family to him.

"Screenwriter," Richard corrected my grandfather. Then he corrected himself. "Would-be screenwriter."

My grandfather frowned. He hated ambiguities.

"I'm trying to sell this screenplay I wrote," Richard ex-plained. "Till then, I'm trying to make ends meet."

Aunt Clara strolled over, her hands up in surrender. "Charles, I'm only coming into enemy territory because I can't wait another minute to meet Lou's sweetheart."

My grandfather scowled at her. "She wants me to take down my moose head and my flying fish," he told me. "They've only been hanging in that den forty-five years. She suddenly doesn't want dead things lying around. Well, fortu-nately, this is my home. Our father willed it to me while she was off gallivanting with the Lord knows whom."

Aunt Clara stuck out her tongue. She had on an old tank suit and madras shorts and was as thin and straight as a girl. She always ate cornflakes for breakfast and an apple for lunch; she thought Americans, my grandfather in particular, ate too much.

"The lake looks beautiful today," I said.

"You can thank Charles for that," Aunt Clara said darkly.

"Why?"

"I finally took care of the beaver, that's why," my grand-father said.

"How?" asked Richard.

"With my .22, that's how."

"Now that's what I call a fair fight," Aunt Clara said.

"You didn't think we should go after the Japs, either."

"That's not true and you know it. I simply didn't think it was necessary to drop the bomb on innocent women and chil-dren."

Sara and Annie had come up from behind and were staring at my grandfather. "Don't worry," I told them. "They're talk-ing about World War II. That was a long time ago."

"I'm only up to the Revolutionary," Annie said. She was a prim eight-year-old, all bones.

"How are you, sweetie?" I said, hugging her.

She wriggled away. "I'm fine," she said, "but Mommy has a headache."

Richard was swinging Sara in circles by her ankles. Her mouth hung wide open. My grandfather watched, his hands in his pockets, still reserving judgment.

"Sara's probably going to throw up," Annie said.

"I like him," Aunt Clara whispered.

"You don't think he's too short for me?"

She laughed. "Honey, at my age, nobody looks too short."

When I heard a car in the driveway, I went up to the house. I found my mother in the kitchen, uncovering the containers of food we'd all brought. "What's this?" she said, holding out my blue glass bowl.

"Potato salad," I said, curling my fingers around a mayonnaised potato chunk.

"Stop!" said my mother. "We're trying to teach the girls not to do things like that. And I told you coleslaw or pasta salad. Charlotte made potato salad. Charlotte always makes the potato salad."

"I made it last year. She made it the year before. Don't you remember, we discussed if I should make the German style again, or regular."

"I'm sure I said coleslaw, but never mind. We've got plenty of other salads." She bent in front of the refrigerator. "Something's going to have to go in the downstairs fridge."

"Where's Charlotte?"

"Resting. She has a headache. She took some Bayer this morning, but it didn't help. I told her Bayer's not the best anymore. I gave her some of that new stuff, what do you call it? Ibuprofen. That's what doctors would bring to desert islands these days."

Before going upstairs to find Charlotte, I stopped in the living room. On the mantel were photographs of three brides — my grandmother, my mother, and Charlotte — all wearing my grandmother's wedding gown. Standing in the same position, looking regally off into nowhere, they could have been triplets.

I wondered if there'd ever be a photograph of me on the mantel. Somehow I couldn't picture Richard in a tux. He'd probably want to wear jeans. Then I couldn't very well wear my grandmother's gown. We wouldn't go together. But if I didn't wear my grandmother's gown, I wouldn't end up on the mantel. My grandfather would make sure of that. Part of me wanted to wear the dress and end up on the mantel with the other women in the family; part of me wished I had the nerve not to.

Upstairs, in the big bed in the front room, the lump that was Charlotte shifted in my direction. Even her head was shrouded by the comforter. "Hi," I whispered from the doorway.

She stuck her head out and opened an eye. "My skull, I swear, is splitting open," she said, her voice hoarse.

"Sorry. I'll go away."

She shook her head, then winced. "Do you know what I mean, like an ax came down and sliced your head in two?"

I shrugged. "I don't really get headaches."

"That's because you have sex," she said.

"What?"

"That's my new theory."

I went over and sat down on the edge of the bed. "That's what happens," I said. "You've been married forever."

"Don't rub it in," she said. "I saw a talk show about it."

"Maybe you should go away together, just the two of you. I'll come stay with the girls."

"That would be cute," she said. "You and Richard playing house." She leaned up on her elbow. "Richard's supposed to sleep in the room next to the girls. Grandpa probably thinks they're some kind of deterrent."

"I'm too terrified to sneak around. I'd die if he heard us."

"Oh, he's just a pussycat," Charlotte said.

"You say that because he likes you."

She shook her head. "He doesn't like anyone."

"Well, he admires you, at least."

She smiled. "Maybe."

My grandfather admired Charlotte because of her nerve. She didn't kowtow to him the way the rest of us did. Even when Charlotte was a kid, she spoke up. Like him, she had opinions and theories on practically everything, including subjects she knew nothing about.

The lake on my grandfather's property was surrounded by purple spiky flowers we'd called phlox until Charlotte took a plant taxonomy course her freshman year in college. "It can't be phlox," she said that summer, her textbook open across her knees. "The *Polemoniaceae* have five flat petals joined at the corolla tube. This flower has only four."

My grandfather had looked up from his tackle box. He was tying flies. "Let me see that," he said.

"And this," Charlotte went on, holding up a delicate orange pocket, "is a touch-me-not."

"Lady's slipper," my grandfather said.

She tapped a color plate. "*Impatiens capensis,* commonly known as touch-me-not," she read.

After examining the book, my grandfather had to admit that Charlotte was right. They worked their way around the property that summer, renaming everything. After that, only the two of them could keep the flowers straight. The rest of us would say, "Run and pick a bunch of those tiny yellow flowers that aren't buttercups."

"Are you coming outside?" I asked Charlotte.

"You don't understand," she said wearily. "Headaches don't go away, one two three. What's everyone doing?"

"I don't know. The girls are diving off the dock with Aunt Clara." I squinted out the window. "Oh, God, Richard and Grandpa are still sitting next to each other."

"I hate when you do that," Charlotte said.

"Do what?"

"Say 'I don't know' in front of everything. It's really annoying. You can see them, so you know what they're doing, so why do you say 'I don't know'?"

"Don't start in on me," I said.

"Tell everyone I'm taking a nap. Make sure nobody comes up here."

"Tell them yourself," I said, turning away from her. When Charlotte and I argued, we sounded like ten-year-olds.

Outside I sat down beside my mother in the semicircle of beach chairs. "Charlotte's in a vicious mood," I said, wriggling against the plastic weave to get comfortable.

"I don't want to hear," my mother said. "Everywhere I look, someone's fighting. I don't understand why people can't get along."

"Do you think I should go rescue Richard?" I asked.

"Let Pop finish with him first." My mother started to get up, then thought better of it. "You know, I hate to side with Pop on anything, but I don't think I've ever seen the lake looking more beautiful."

"I always think of Charlotte's wedding when I'm out here," I said.

"Don't remind me," my mother said. "Will you ever forget those geese? What a mess that was."

The night before Charlotte's wedding, a flock of geese had landed on the lake. In the morning, we chased them away, raked their droppings off the lawn, and hosed the dock. "Maybe that's a lucky omen," I remember my mother saying. "The weather will hold out."

But my grandfather said, "It's no honor having your pond chosen as a pit stop."

My mother had been afraid he wouldn't allow the wedding to be at his house if he knew Charlotte was pregnant, so we were sworn to secrecy. It wasn't easy to hide; Charlotte was getting big. She wore my grandmother's gown let out as far as it would go.

My great-grandmother had made the dress, ivory satin buoyed by tulle. For Charlotte, my mother dismantled the layers of the skirt and had the lace repaired where the heel of her pump had torn a hole at her own wedding. "Your father and I were doing the polka," she told Charlotte and me, the day she took the gown from the cedar chest. "We got too close to the cake table and practically turned the whole thing over."

Every time she fastened Charlotte into the dress for fittings, she would say, "Stand up straight, and don't you dare gain another ounce."

"There's not much I can do about that," Charlotte muttered.

Minutes before the ceremony, she was hunched over the bathroom sink, retching, the dress crumpled around her knees. While my mother patted Charlotte's back, I stood guard at the door.

The dress was so stiff and heavy that once in it, Charlotte couldn't sit down. My mother propped her up against a wall and patted rouge on her pale cheeks. Charlotte munched a saltine. "I know what I should have done with this baby," she suddenly said.

When my mother hauled off and slapped her, Charlotte lost her balance and slid down the wall. "Help her up," my mother commanded me. "Quick, before the dress wrinkles."

I rearranged the folds. A patch on Charlotte's cheek turned bright pink. "This isn't the way it's supposed to be," she sobbed.

"That's for sure," my mother said from across the room, where she'd retreated.

My father tapped on the door. "All set?" he called. We should have been outside already, beginning our procession. When no one answered, he peered in. "What the aitch?" He quickly closed the door behind him. "I don't know what happened, and I don't want to know," he announced. "We've got a hundred-plus people waiting down there, so you better get a move on. Liz, go stall everyone."

Charlotte was crying steadily by then. I dabbed her face with a washcloth. "Someone, do something!" my father said. "You've got five minutes."

"Lou, go help Daddy downstairs," my mother commanded me, taking the wet cloth away. "Come here, baby," she said, pulling Charlotte into her arms.

"Where's Mommy?" Sara cried, running up from the lake, wet and panting.

"She's taking a nap," my mother said from her beach chair. "Come cool me off."

Sara put her arms around my mother's neck. For a moment, they held each other, cheek to cheek. "You're better than any air conditioner," my mother said.

"Sara, how's school?" I asked. She'd just finished first grade.

Sara giggled. "We don't go to school in the summer, dummy."

"Don't call Aunt Lou dummy," said my mother.

"But it was a dumb question, wasn't it?"

I tried again. "I meant how *was* school?"

"My teacher has silver hair," Sara said. "Her hair went silver because her heart was broken."

My mother and I laughed. "Who told you that?" I said.

"Mommy," said Sara. "Can I go wake her up?"

"Yes," I said. "Go wake her up." Sara skipped up the hill to the house.

"Charlotte thinks I raised you girls to be meek," my mother said. "But I think hers are getting fresh." She leaned forward. "Phil!"

My father and Sam had gone out fishing in one of the canoes. My father waved to my mother and me. "Cover your shoulders," my mother called to him. "You're getting burnt."

She turned to me. "I know he's getting burnt. Richard should watch out, too. People think that just because it's not the beach, the sun's not strong."

When I went over to warn Richard, he was telling my grandfather about the trouble filmmakers have coming up with money to make their movies. I could tell from the way his arms were folded that my grandfather had decided not to like Richard. He was probably storing up Richard's imperfections to report back to the rest of the family. Sometimes I worried about being descended from someone as mean as my grandfather.

"It's too late," he said cheerfully, when I handed Richard his T-shirt. "Those shoulders are fried." My grandfather, who had on sneakers, socks, khakis, a long-sleeved shirt buttoned at the wrists, and a visored cap would never have dreamed of exposing more than his hands to the sun.

Richard looked surprised. He'd probably figured he had my grandfather eating out of the palm of his hand by then.

"His shoulders are not fried," I said. "By morning, they'll be tan."

Ordinarily, my grandfather would have made sure he had the final word on the subject, but just then, Charlotte came floating down the hillside. She had on dark glasses and a new black bathing suit with cutouts on her sides and stomach. Even though it was only the beginning of the summer, she was tan from working in her garden. She was always tan before the rest of the world.

"Hi, everyone," she said. "Hi, Richard."

Richard stood up and went over and kissed her cheek. "You look ravishing," he said. He always seemed to go out of his way to compliment people.

"I was thinking," Charlotte said, sitting down in a free chair. "What if we eat in the arbor tonight, instead of dragging everything all the way down here?" When no one said anything, she went on, "It would save our legs. And the arbor would look lovely with paper lanterns."

"But, Charlotte, we've always eaten by the lake on Fourth of July," my mother said.

"Well, we can change tradition, can't we?" Charlotte said.

"If you change tradition, it's not tradition anymore," said my mother.

"If you want to change something," Aunt Clara said, "I vote to use paper cups and plates. I don't know who started the fool tradition of having a picnic with china and crystal."

"I believe I started that fool tradition," my grandfather said.

"Let's take a walk," I whispered to Richard. It would take half an hour to walk around the lake, longer if we stopped for a swim on the far side. By then, the argument would have subsided.

Once we were out of earshot, I said, "I'm sorry to drag you up here."

"What happens when your grandfather gets mad? Does someone get killed?" Richard asked.

After we'd gone a ways, he paused and turned to look back at the group. From a distance, it looked like any old family gathering. He flipped the lens cap off his camera and peered through the aperture. "What do you think they're talking about right now?" he asked.

"You."

Startled, he lowered the camera. He fitted the cap back on the lens.

When we crossed the bridge over the stream that fed the lake, we had to choose between two paths. One circled the lake; the other broke off into the woods. We took the second, which led to an enormous pine, the oldest tree on the property, according to my grandfather. Its branches hung so wide and low that after ducking under we could stand beneath them and be hidden.

Richard turned around in the dappled light. Facing me again, he smiled.

When we were kids, Charlotte and I were always on the

lookout for hiding places. We loved coming to the Berkshires because my grandfather's house was full of nooks and crannies, and on his property were hedges and the woods. Our favorite hiding place was beneath this tree. We supplied it with buried matches, jars for collecting fireflies and worms, sticks for swords in case we had to defend ourselves against intruders.

I was telling Richard this as we lay on the moss, when Charlotte called through the trees. "I should have known," I said, reluctantly untangling myself.

Charlotte stooped to clear the outer branches. "I knew you'd bring Richard here," she said to me. She looked around. "This was your side, and this was mine, remember?"

"How's your head68he?" I said in a not exactly welcoming voice.

"All gone," she said brightly. "Richard, would you believe that at the end of our two weeks here we were still white from spending all our time under this tree?"

"Did you win?" Richard asked. "Are we going to have dinner in the arbor?"

"Oh, I had no hopes of winning that argument," Charlotte said. "I just like to get them riled up. It's always the same here. Don't you want to shake them sometimes, Lou? There are times I say anything, just to get them started."

"I hate when everyone's fighting," I said.

Her laugh reverberated in the shade of the tree. "I love fights, don't you, Richard? I know you do — that's why you want to make movies. You like conflict and drama, I know you do."

She was right, of course, but Richard said, "I like it when it happens naturally. I don't believe in making it happen."

"You're like Sam," she said. "He'd kill me if he knew what I started back there."

"I'm taking a swim," I announced, turning my back on the two of them.

By the shore of the lake, I waited and waited, but neither Charlotte nor Richard appeared. Richard couldn't help being interested in Charlotte, I told myself; she was an alarming, perplexing person. "She's material," he'd say later. I knew I would forgive him. It was Charlotte I couldn't always forgive.

"I'm trying to reach her," Richard explained to me that night after everyone else had gone to bed and I finally had a chance to ask him what he and Charlotte had talked about under the tree. The two of us were the only human flesh outdoors, and the mosquitos were making a meal of us.

"What exactly are you trying to reach?"

Richard slapped at a bug and didn't answer.

Suddenly, in what I'd always thought of as music, I heard a din of bullfrogs and crickets, something rustling through the bushes, pebbles on the beach scraping against each other like fingernails on a chalkboard.

"Mommy wants to know if you two are being good," Sara called out the window.

"Tell her to mind her own business," I said.

"Hey, pooch," said Richard, patting a strange dog who'd appeared out of nowhere.

"Lou?" called my mother.

"Yeah?"

"Turn out the lights when you come in. Pop'll have a fit if they're left on."

"Okay."

"Hi, Grandma," Sara called.

"Hi, sweetie. Aren't you in bed yet?"

"Almost," said Sara.

"Sara, come in. You're going to fall," said Charlotte.

"I can't sleep," Sara whined. "I have sunburn."

"You do not. I checked," Charlotte said. "Just lie down and close your eyes and think nice things."

"Like what?" Sara asked.

"Death-defying tightrope acts," Charlotte suggested.

From the other side of the house, my grandfather shouted, "Whose dog is that?"

"I don't know," I said.

"It's probably the Talbot woman over the hill. Clara! Call that Talbot woman and tell her I want that mutt off my property."

"Come on," I whispered to Richard.

We stood up and started toward the lake. "Where're you going?" called Charlotte, poking her head out again.

"Honey, leave them alone," I heard Sam say.

tHree

SOON AFTER that summer, I was made music director at a girls' school on the Upper East Side. There I taught music appreciation and ran the glee club.

A few years went by. For the most part, I was content. Sometimes, though, Charlotte and I would get talking, and she'd say, "Remember how I wanted to save the world, and you wanted to be the next Horowitz?" We'd laugh, but for days afterward, in the middle of a rehearsal or a class, I'd find myself thinking, "Just what exactly does this amount to?" And when, after all his years of struggling, Richard found a producer for his movie, I was happy for him but wished I could figure out what to do with my own life. Things began to seem hardly more than satisfactory. I was still hanging on to my apartment. Though I'd been at my job three years, I'd never stopped considering it temporary.

The evening in late October just before Halloween when Sam appeared on my doorstep, I'd been giving myself a lecture. "You've got a nice boyfriend, a nice family, a decent job. Quit complaining. You had a bad day, that's all."

That morning, Lydia, one of my altos, had cried that she wouldn't be an alto anymore because I'd switched her best friend to the soprano section, and after school, the principal had called me in to his office to question a song I'd put on the Christmas program we were beginning to rehearse. He read aloud to me from the page of lyrics I'd sent him, then asked if I didn't think the song had a negative message. Without bothering to disagree with him, I said I'd choose another song. He laid the sheet of paper down, disappointed. He liked to discuss the most minute details, but I was too discouraged to argue. Before leaving his office, I told him I needed a new cymbal. "Have you filled out a requisition form?" he asked me. He was a stickler for rules and regulations. I sighed and told him I'd fill out his form.

That afternoon, I walked home from the subway, dragging my feet. I had two piano students to face before dinner. After that, nothing. Richard was in L.A. while his movie was being filmed. He'd been floating for the past few months. In bed, he'd say, "Pinch me. Tell me this is really happening." I'd pinch him, hard, anything to bring him back down to earth. One time he said, "This is your success, too. Who else would have read all those drafts?" He could tell I felt left out.

When I reached my building, my downstairs neighbor Mrs. Rapetti was waiting for me on the front stoop. "Vinnie's sleeping," she said. "You tell those kids to step quiet and don't bang the keys." Vinnie was her forty-year-old retarded son.

"They'll bang no matter what I say."

She glared. "How often does Vinnie fall asleep in the afternoon? Don't I deserve a rest?"

We'd been through this before. "This is my job," I said. "If I don't make the money, I can't pay the rent, and who knows who you'll end up with — some big man with thumping feet who brings loud women home."

"All right, all right." She squinted at me. "You tell them to walk quiet," she warned.

"I will," I promised.

"Richard's not back?"

I shook my head.

"You come down later, we'll play cards."

"Maybe," I said.

"You don't eat right. You come down, I'll fix you a glass of red wine to thicken your blood."

Climbing the stairs, I thought once again about giving up

my apartment. My lease was up for renewal. Last time, I'd been able to get away with telling Richard we hadn't known each other long enough, but that wouldn't work now. And he'd already told me he didn't mind my giving piano lessons at his place.

"Your apartment isn't big enough to breathe in" was how Richard always began his argument for why I should move in with him. He lived in a loft, over two thousand square feet with windows facing south and east and west. It was high enough up that we could see water towers and rooftops across the city, and the sky. The place was rough — the floors sagged and the kitchen and bathroom equipment was second-hand stuff he'd picked up cheaply and installed himself, but the windows were always crystal clear. Richard would sit on the sill, outside the glass, to polish them, while I held tight to his legs.

I wasn't expecting Sam that evening. If Charlotte was coming into the city for dinner or a movie, she and Sam sometimes arranged to meet at my place, but this time, she hadn't called to warn me. For once I didn't mind the intrusion. I'd had to scold both of my piano students for not practicing; there was nothing in the refrigerator for supper but some leftover mu shu pork; I missed Richard.

Sam followed me into the living room. He stopped and stared at the photographs on the wall above the piano — pictures of Charlotte and the kids, mostly. "Mom just sent me new ones from the summer," I said, taking the envelope from the mantel. "The girls are really getting big."

In one picture Annie was wearing her first bikini; in another Sara had zinc oxide smeared over her nose and lips. Sam shuffled through the stack twice before he finally said in a rush, "Charlotte's gone."

"Gone?"

Sam just stood there, clutching the photographs.

For a moment I fantasized that Charlotte would come to

live with me. But the next moment, I realized that if she was gone, she'd left me, too. I'd seen her that weekend. I'd spoken to her the night before. She hadn't said anything about leaving.

"She'll be back," I said, but Sam shook his head. "Of course she will," I went on. "She probably needed time to think. Maybe she wanted to wake up alone for once. Maybe she's tired of spending her whole life in that tiny town. You should move back to the city. The girls are big enough."

But Sam kept shaking his head, and I could tell he wasn't paying attention. "Stop wagging your head, for God's sake," I said. "Where did she go?" He was as bad as Charlotte about holding back information.

When he finally pulled himself together and told me, I went into the bedroom to get my jacket. On the dresser was a lone onyx earring. I dropped it into my pocket, and for the next few days I felt the rounded edges of the earring whenever I reached for my gloves. Charlotte had died that afternoon in a car accident. Apparently, she'd swerved to avoid an avalanche of pumpkins falling from a flatbed truck on its way to the city, and had driven smack into a telephone pole.

The first two weeks after Charlotte's death, the girls and Sam and I stayed at my parents' house. It was my mother's idea, and I didn't protest. Richard wasn't back yet and when I'd gone home to pick up some clothes, Mrs. Rapetti almost smothered me with a big, damp hug.

Sam went along with my mother's suggestion, too. You could have set him down anywhere, it would have been all the same to him.

My mother orchestrated us as if she were a symphony conductor, prompting us with chores and errands. The girls and I baked more oatmeal cookies than any of us could eat. My father cleaned closets, or rather, emptied them, then put everything back in the same place. Only Sam didn't join in. He just sat on the couch.

Richard kept calling from Los Angeles, promising to get

away for a day or two. "I think I can slip out of here tonight. Take this down," he'd say, and rattle off a flight number and arrival time. But just as I'd be about to leave for the airport to pick him up, there'd be another call. "Lou, forgive me. I can't do it. Later in the week, I promise."

Later never came. The last time Richard called to tell me what flight he'd be on, I got all the way out to the airport, but when I reached the gate, I heard myself being paged. My mother had left a message: "Come home." She told me later that Richard was anxious to explain what had kept him from coming this time, but I didn't bother calling him back.

One afternoon, in the middle of the third week, my mother laid down her sponge. She and I had been cleaning the pantry. "We've got to stop this," she said. "We have to carry on, for the girls' sakes. They have to move back into that house. We're going to have to find someone."

Someone. It sounded ominous. A stranger, she was talking about, to take Charlotte's place, to brush Sara's hair and get meals on the table, to be there.

"We'll have to go to an agency," my mother went on, picking up her sponge and scrubbing a stubborn spot.

"An agency?"

"We have to be realistic."

She was right, of course. We couldn't keep on baking and cleaning as if we were getting ready for a party.

"A live-in person," my mother said. "Sam travels so much. Someone kind and understanding and young enough, someone who doesn't have kids of her own, someone —"

"Maybe I can do it," I said.

My mother stopped her cleaning and stared at me. I was as surprised as she. But I didn't take it back. "For a little while," I went on. "Until we find the right person. Until we get our bearings."

The more I thought about it, the more it started to make sense. I'd take a leave of absence from school. It would be better for the girls. It would be better all around.

The next morning, I went in to the city to meet with the

principal of my school. I remembered to thank him for the flower arrangement he'd sent.

"We wanted to do something," he said. "Everyone chipped in."

I explained that I needed more time off. "Someone's got to take care of the girls till we find a housekeeper," I said. "My mother's too old to be chasing after them."

"Well," said the principal, nodding slowly. "We did have that substitute in when you had the flu last year."

"Tell her we need a new cymbal," I said.

"Did you ever find time to fill out a requisition form?"

I shook my head. "Tell her the altos need work, but the sopranos are strong. Tell her to remind Miss Mosely to slow down. She likes to show off how fast she can play."

I came close that moment to changing my mind. We were on the verge of becoming an award-winning glee club. These were crucial months. My altos could go either way, especially with the Gershwin.

"I'm sure it'll work out," the principal said. But as I stood to shake his hand, I didn't see how that would be possible.

After leaving the principal, I took the subway downtown. At my stop, I got off and headed home. Knowing I wouldn't be seeing them for a while, I paid attention to the landmarks of my neighborhood — the arch at the head of Washington Square Park, where Richard and I used to meet before going to the pool; a leather boutique whose mannequins wore only studded belts and cowboy boots; an Italian pastry shop with an enormous cardboard wedding cake in the window. Along the way, I stopped by the post office and arranged for my mail to be forwarded to Charlotte's address, and at the bank, I transferred my savings into my checking account, so I'd have enough money.

In the years I'd been in the city, most of my friends had moved — to larger apartments, to their boyfriends' places, back on their own again. But my apartment was the very same one I'd spotted in *The Village Voice* classifieds the summer after college. One bedroom, new kitchen, convenient, $275. The bathtub had been the clincher; all the other apartments I'd looked at were equipped with only stall showers.

When I got home, I packed more clothes and a few treasures I couldn't live without — the teapot that played "Lara's Theme" when tipped, an old silver hand mirror. I looked around one last time. Most everything I owned was old and worn, except for the harvest table, which I kept folded and covered with a tablecloth. Refinishing it had been a mistake. Smooth and shiny, it was totally out of place with my beloved junk.

I closed the piano and locked the door, then went downstairs to give Mrs. Rapetti a key and a list of instructions about my plants. She hugged me and cried and said that she and Vinnie were going to miss me, but I just wanted to get out of there as fast as I could.

The next morning I telephoned Richard in L.A., waking him up in his hotel room. I'd purposely called him at a time when he wouldn't be entirely alert.

"Wait, hold on, what?" he said, coming to. "You're going to what?"

"It's only temporary."

"But what about your glee club?"

"They'll manage."

"What about me?"

"You're not here," I reminded him.

"Don't you think we should sit down and discuss this calmly?" Richard said.

"I am calm," I told him. "And I've already made up my mind."

When we moved back to Charlotte's house, I slept in the guest room, and Sam slept downstairs on the living room couch. He wouldn't go near the room he'd shared with Charlotte. I tried to run the household exactly as she had, and the girls pointed out anything I did wrong.

The day we moved, my mother had a long talk with Sam. She told him everyone was trying and he had to try, too. If anything, her talk made things worse. The best Sam could do was play the part of a father. Coming through the door, he would shout, "It's me!" He'd never done that before. At the sound of his voice, the girls came running and leaped into his arms. They'd never done that before, either. Charlotte used to have to make them stop what they were doing to greet their father.

At the table, we were overly polite. "Please pass the string beans, thank you. Please pass the steak." Even when we could have reached the salt and pepper by barely touching a sleeve or a wrist, we asked.

We ate voraciously, seconds and thirds. We ate for eating's sake, not out of hunger but to feel our jaws and teeth work. The girls drank their milk and ate their vegetables with no fuss.

Those first few weeks, Sam and I raided the wine cellar. We drank everything, even dessert wines that should have been sipped and good champagnes that he and Charlotte had been saving for celebrations. And after the girls went to bed, although we'd already had enough, Sam would say, "How about a little something?"

I'd pour the brandy while he ran outside for logs with just a bathrobe on over his clothes. He built his fires carefully, propping up the bottom log so it could breathe, adding kindling at the proper angles, balancing the smaller log on top. Not at all the way Charlotte used to do it. She was an expert at short cuts. She taped hems instead of bothering with the sewing machine. Her fires were intense but short-lived, just paper burning, really.

At first, sitting together in front of the fire, Sam would entertain me with anecdotes about his job or quiz me about my life, as if I'd just stopped by for a visit. But more and more often, we'd sit in uncomfortable silence, not knowing where to begin. There was no precedent for our situation. We'd been alone together before, but Charlotte was always in the background. We'd never had to figure out how we really felt about each other.

One evening, after Sam had arranged another log on the fire, he dropped down beside me on the couch, and stretching his arms overhead, accidentally grazed my hair. "Sorry," he said, jumping up. He poked at the logs, then sat down, this time in an armchair.

"So," he said briskly. "How's Richard?"

"Still working on his movie."

Sam stared into the fire. "I'd love to make a movie," he said.

"I thought you loved your work." Although I'd had it explained several times, what Sam actually did remained a mystery to me.

"Oh, I do," he said. "I mean, you can't have everything, can you?" He swirled his glass so the liquid lapped the sides. "Take a nice secure position with room to grow. That's what my father always said."

Sam reached for the brandy, then changed his mind and set his glass down. "Play it safe," he said. "I tried. Back in college, I never did acid because I was afraid for my babies. Who else was worrying about babies back then?"

He leaned forward. "But you know what? The things I've been afraid of all my life never happen. I used to be afraid someone was going to break into my gym locker at school and steal my clothes and I'd have to make it home in a towel. I used to think Charlotte's heel was going to get stuck in a subway grate. And remember that day at the track? When you came running up to me, I was sure something had happened to the baby. I could have kicked myself, taking a woman that pregnant to the races in ninety-degree heat."

The moment he paused, I stood up and reached for the glasses. I didn't want to hear another word.

But Sam was finished. He swung his legs onto the coffee table and closed his eyes. Out the front end of his right sock poked his big toe. Knowing I'd let him down somehow, I went and got a blanket and draped it over him. I promised myself that in the morning, I'd go through his sock drawer and mend the ones with holes.

After that night, Sam started coming home later and later, and when he finally arrived, he'd go straight to the kitchen. "There's a lasagna in the fridge," I'd call from the living room, but then I'd hear a cabinet opening and cereal rustling into a bowl. I made a point of going upstairs by the time he was finished eating.

When Christmas came, I didn't consult with Sam about what to buy the girls. I winged it and charged everything to Charlotte's credit cards. I forged her signature, crossing the double *t*'s with one swift stroke. Staring the salespeople straight in the eye, I dared anyone to challenge me.

four

AT FIRST, my mother came over every day with meat loaves and chocolate chip cookies. Annie and Sara clung to her. They knew her better than they knew me; plus she was old. Even if it meant hanging around the house until she arrived, they waited to ask her permission to do things. She'd tell them to ask me, but she'd add, "I'm sure it's okay," or "I don't know if Aunt Lou will like that," giving me hints about how to answer.

The day after New Year's, though, my parents went to Florida. The last thing my mother wanted to do was leave us, but my father needed to get away. He hadn't been himself since Charlotte died.

Actually, he hadn't been himself since the June before Charlotte's accident, when he retired as commissioner of the fire department. The morning after his retirement party, he wandered around the house, then decided to go jogging. Just a block from home, one of his knees went out. While he was convalescing, he tried to label the snapshots in the family photo albums, but he didn't recognize all the faces and had to keep pestering my mother.

Finally, he hit on a hobby — making useful things out of junk. He put together a lamp with an old carburetor for a base. He fashioned wastepaper baskets out of laminated cornflakes boxes, and pencil holders from toilet paper rolls. But when Charlotte died, he cleared off his workbench. "What was I thinking of?" he'd said to my mother. "I could have been spending time with things that matter."

Even with Charlotte gone, my mother carried on as usual, cooking and cleaning and yakking on the phone. She'd jump into the car at a moment's notice to have lunch with a friend, pick someone up from the train station, take advantage of the final day of a sale. But my father was lost. He had nothing to distract him from his thoughts. He had no job. He had no hobbies. He wasn't a reader or a crossword puzzle type. Current events depressed him.

In Florida he took naps, while my mother cooked shrimp a dozen different ways and shined the sliding glass doors of the apartment that she and my father had bought for their old age. Accustomed to lakes, she hated how sandy everything got at the beach despite all her efforts. She went south for my father's sake.

That January she telephoned every single morning from Florida to make sure the girls and I were okay. "How's Dad?" I asked one Friday, after she'd gone through her usual battery of questions. I was in the kitchen, fixing breakfast for the girls. Sam had been away all week on business.

"I'm watching your father out the window as we speak," my mother said. "He's doing his laps in the ocean today. I'm supposed to holler if I see any sharks."

"What's he going to say when he sees this phone bill?"

"He's not going to," she said. "When you get married, remind me to teach you a few tricks."

Even if we hadn't been on the telephone, my mother would have heard Sara's shriek all the way down in Florida. It sounded like a dog with his tail trapped in a door. "Hang on," I said, and ran to the foot of the stairs. "Girls?" I called. There was silence. "That's more like it," I said.

"Don't you even want to know what we're fighting about?" Sara called.

"No."

"Don't let Annie bully Sara," my mother said when I picked up the phone again. "That's what happens when siblings are so close in age. That's what happened to you. I should have waited longer in between. But back then we didn't worry about the psychological repercussions. I told Charlotte to wait a little longer."

"Everything's under control," I said. Holding the receiver in the crook of my neck, I buttered toast. In Florida, my mother was squeezing oranges. We worked in silence for a few minutes.

When Annie slouched in, I moved the receiver and kissed her head, then I wiped my mouth. Her cropped hair was sticky from the gel she used to make it stand on end. "Tell Grandma everything's fine," I said.

"You mean lie?" She took the phone. "Everything's fine, Grandma." She listened. "No, Daddy had to stay over another day. He's coming home tonight. What?" She covered the mouthpiece and asked me what was for supper.

"I have no idea."

"Lamb chops," Annie said into the phone. "Yes, I know Aunt Lou is a saint."

"I wanted to wear my pink jeans today," she told me after she hung up. "I wanted Isaac to see me in them." Isaac was her new boyfriend, an eighth-grader.

"I haven't had a chance to hem them yet," I said. "I'll do it soon, I promise."

"You've been promising for two weeks already."

Sara skipped in. She rolled her eyes, making the pupils disappear, and started swaying. "I'm possessed!" she cried.

"You look like the girl in the movie last night," Annie said.

I knew I shouldn't have let them watch it. Sam didn't approve of scary movies. Once he'd suggested getting rid of the TV altogether. "It's a Pandora's box," he told Charlotte. But he never said things like that anymore. He left all the decisions to me.

"Annie, better hurry," I said. "Where's your jacket?" It was already eight. If she missed the bus, I'd have to drive her to the junior high on the other side of town.

"My jeans, don't forget!" she called, as she ran out.

"Do you think I might have been a dinosaur in one of my past lives?" Sara said when she heard Annie slam the door and knew that she had me to herself. She still walked to the elementary school.

"Anything's possible," I said, handing her a piece of toast. She rocked her chair back. "Do you think human beings are going extinct?" I shook my head. "Do you think robots will take over?"

"No. Why? Do you want them to?"

She shrugged. "I wouldn't mind."

"Better eat that and get going," I said.

"I've got a pain, here," she said, touching her stomach.

"You've already missed school once this week. Your father will have a fit when he finds out."

"Don't tell him," she said. "Isn't it easier when I'm around? Aren't I a big help?"

"Yes, but we're not supposed to take the easy way out," I said.

"Why not?"

"Because adversity builds character."

"What does that mean?" she asked.

"One more question, and you're going to school."

She blew me kisses, then knelt, stretched her arms overhead, and touched the floor with her forehead. "I'm thanking Allah," she said.

I didn't know where she'd picked that up from. Some cartoon, probably. My view of television was different from Sam's. I didn't think it was nearly as damaging as life.

We had a list of errands that day — the five and ten for thread to match Annie's jeans, the Chinese laundry, the supermarket. Sara and I argued every step of the way. She wanted her father's shirts folded around cardboard, not hung on hangers.

"When they fold them, they just iron in the wrinkles," I said.

"I need the cardboard for drawing," she insisted.

At the supermarket, we stopped at the meat counter, and I asked the butcher for a few pounds of chopped chuck. Sara shook her head. "You can get sirloin for just pennies more," she told me.

I glanced back at the butcher. "She's right," he said.

When I ordered the lamb for dinner, though, Sara didn't butt in. She stared through the glass display window at the row of chops lying on a bloody sheet of butcher paper. Lamb chops had been Charlotte's favorite. She'd eat three herself; then, when everyone else was finished, she'd gather up the bones and chew the marrow from each one.

After the supermarket, Sara made me stop at the stationery store but wouldn't tell me why or let me come in with her. When she got back to the car, she showed me a diary with a tiny gold key. "Santa Claus forgot," she said.

For lunch, we went to McDonald's. I ordered a hamburger, French fries, and a Coke. Sara ordered nothing. "Mom said you have to be crazy to eat here," she said. "Everything but the milk shakes is practically poison."

"We're not much alike, your mother and I."

Sara looked closely at me. "Her nose wasn't bumpy. Her hair was even all around."

At the library we separated, like enemies retreating after a battle. I headed for the adult stacks, Sara for the children's corner. She picked out six books, the limit. At home, she usually read while Annie tried out new hairstyles or played an imaginary electric guitar, and Sam sat by himself in the study.

When I handed Charlotte's library card to the librarian, Sara asked me, "When are you going to get your own?"

"I'm not going to be here forever," I said.

That quieted Sara, but in my heart, I wasn't sure if what I'd said was true. The longer I stayed, the less I could imagine going back. When Richard called, all I felt was weary. "When are you going home?" he'd ask, without a "hello" or "how are you." Instead of being touched by his urgency, I wanted to hang up on him.

My principal was far more understanding. When I called to tell him I wouldn't be back this semester, he said, "You take your time. Things are working out nicely with Miss Kendall."

But after my conversation with him, I felt uneasy. Didn't he or any of my kids miss me?

On weekends, the employment agency would send over applicants for the position of housekeeper. Most of them I didn't even bother introducing to Sam. "The girls don't eat peanut butter and jelly," I told a plump, kindly-looking woman with a brogue.

"Well, they'll soon be learning to," she said.

"Sara needs the light on to fall asleep," I told a woman who'd taught the Montessóri method for ten years.

"We can't have her getting into a bad habit like that, now can we?" she said.

Only one in the whole lot seemed remotely possible. In a red down coat, loafers, and no makeup, the woman looked like someone who might actually live in Charlotte's house. After talking with her for a few minutes, I brought her outside, where Sam was sitting in the cold.

From the kitchen window, I watched them, side by side on the terrace steps. The yard was gray except for the woman's coat. Her legs were stretched in front of her on the faded straw-colored grass, and she nodded as she spoke.

The girls came downstairs to investigate. "Who's she?" asked Annie. Sara climbed onto the counter and grabbed my neck in a gentle stranglehold. Her wrists smelled of too many perfumes sprayed on at once. She could never learn to keep her hands off the things she wanted.

When Sam and the woman in the red coat came in, I introduced her to the girls, then told her I'd be in touch. "Well?" I said, once she was gone.

Sam shrugged and went over and opened the refrigerator door.

"What was wrong with her?" I said.

"She was wearing nylons with loafers for one thing," Annie said.

"Her eyes were squinty," said Sara.

Annie nodded.

"She pronounced my name wrong," Sara went on.

"She was too skinny," Annie said.

After I rejected that applicant, the man at the employment agency asked me to come see him. "I've sent you my best girls," he said when we were face to face. "Not one of them was good enough. Just what exactly are you looking for?"

Charlotte had arranged to play the piano at the local ballet school, in exchange for lessons for the girls. After she died, I took over. On Fridays, I usually picked Annie and Sara up after school so we'd be on time.

That afternoon, while Sara and I waited in front of the junior high for Annie, Sara opened and shut the cover of her new diary. "Annie probably had to stay after again," she finally said. Lately, Annie had been getting in trouble for talking back.

I went inside to check. The principal's secretary looked at the list posted on the office door. "Annie's not in detention," she said. "Is she a member of the chess club?"

When I got back to the car, Sara was gone.

I drove slowly toward home, trying not to get upset. On the way I spotted Sara's blue jacket, but I didn't stop. This had happened before. She just wanted to be left alone.

Sara came in twenty minutes after me and silently trudged upstairs to change into her ballet things. When it was almost time to go, I wrote Annie a note, saying we'd left without her. I half expected to find that she'd gotten to ballet by herself. I called to Sara to get a move on, but there was no answer. I called again, then went up after her.

I opened the door to the girls' room and saw Sara lying on her bed in her leotard and tights, scribbling in her diary. Its key was hanging around her neck. What she didn't know was that the lock was useless; her father had figured out how to pick the old one with a straight pin. I caught him at it one afternoon when my mother had the girls. I argued that Sara had a right to her privacy, but Sam kept reading. "I want to know what's going on in that head of hers," he said. "There're other ways of finding out," I said. "Ever heard of asking?" I wanted to get us into a fight. That would be better, I thought, than the tension between us. But Sam just slid the diary under Sara's mattress where she always hid it and left the room.

"I'm almost done," Sara said, not bothering to look up.

I sat down on Annie's bed to wait. Those same beds had been Charlotte's and mine. Our wallpaper, after many arguments, was violets — Charlotte's first choice. A framed Declaration of Independence had hung over my bed; above hers was the Lord's Prayer.

Once Charlotte suggested we trade places for a night, to see what it felt like. It was okay as long as the light was on, just strange, because everything was backward. The rocking chair was in the mirror instead of the lavender lamp.

But in the dark, I couldn't sleep. Charlotte's pillow smelled strange; she was always trying on our mother's perfumes. I wanted to go back to my own bed, but Charlotte was already snoring.

In the morning, I wakened, startled, and gashed my forehead on the corner of the night table. I bled briefly but enough that the sheets had to be changed, and Charlotte said, "Thanks a lot for ruining my bed."

Ballet classes were held in the basement of Our Lady of Miracles, where weddings took place, and the annual Women's Club ball. It was an enormous room. No matter how loud I played, I could never fill its corners. By the time Sara and I got there, the other girls were already lined up at the barre, practicing their pliés, and I hurried over to the piano, an old baby grand.

The teacher called herself "Madame," but she was really just Nan Gordon from next door. I used to make fun of her to Charlotte. Once I held up a piece of Monopoly money and said, "That accent of hers is about as genuine as this ten dollar bill." That began one of our worst fights. I hadn't realized that Charlotte and Nan were becoming friends — trading volumes of Simone de Beauvoir and recipes for perfect madeleines. After that, I was careful about what I said.

"You're tearing through that piece," Nan Gordon cried now, shaking her head at me. No strands escaped her perfect bun. In the summer, she and Charlotte used to French-braid each other's hair.

I slowed the tempo. I was getting rusty. I hadn't touched the piano at Charlotte's house except to dust.

The class glissaded across the floor — all but Sara, who skidded into the girl next to her, then stopped short. She had trouble coordinating her arms with her feet. Soon her face was patchy and red. Every time she made a mistake, I did, too. Madame Gordon was frowning when she finally clapped her hands and cried, "Toe shoes on, mesdemoiselles!"

When we got home, I parked the car in the garage, and Sara and I walked across the lawn to the front door. The ground was lumpy and hard; we hadn't had any snow yet. Last winter there'd been none at all, and the girls were disappointed. But not as disappointed as Charlotte, who loved the cold and snow. In the winter she wore a long, forest green cape, even when she went skating, even when our mother said, "You look like a pine tree in that."

It was almost dark, and after checking for Annie inside, I stood on the front steps, scanning the road in both directions. I told myself she was most likely at a friend's house, but by now I should have started calling around to find her. All my years of observing Charlotte hadn't prepared me for this. I felt like a private suddenly promoted to general of the entire army.

Sara pranced in the doorway to keep warm. "When's Annie coming home?" she asked.

"Soon," I said. I looked at my watch. It was almost five. I wondered if Sam was going to make it home tonight. He'd telephoned the night before to say he'd taken a cab to the airport right after his final meeting, and was on line for the shuttle, when suddenly, without intending to, he'd retraced his steps back to the hotel.

"Get a good night's sleep," I'd instructed him over the phone. "You'll feel better in the morning."

He didn't answer. "All right, you won't feel better," I said, "but you still have to come home."

Sara let go of the storm door and took off down the front walk, soundless in her ballet slippers. Someone was coming. I squinted and saw that it was Annie. I sat down and stuffed my hands in my pockets. I'd forgotten my gloves.

When Sara reached the sidewalk, she stopped short. I knew why. She didn't want to appear too eager. That way, if Annie decided to ignore her, she wouldn't lose face. At calculations like that, I was an expert. If Charlotte smoked a cigarette out the window when she came home from a date, it meant she didn't want to talk. If she didn't comment on something new I was wearing, it meant she'd soon ask to borrow it. It was a whole other language.

"Aunt Lou won't come in," Sara told Annie when they were standing in front of me.

Annie shrugged. "It's a free country," she said.

"Did you forget about ballet?" I asked her.

She shook her head. "I didn't feel like it. I went over to Isaac's and listened to music, instead."

"What if no one did anything unless they felt like it?" I said. "What if you were waiting for Isaac and he didn't show up because he didn't feel like it?"

"He'd never do that." Annie squeezed past me and stepped inside. Without another glance in my direction, Sara hurried after her.

They could be nasty. At times I had to control myself to keep from lashing out and hurting back. I had to count to ten and remind myself that they were just kids.

When Sara poked her head out ten minutes later, I was still sitting on the front steps. Even my hair was frozen. "How long do you cook a baked potato?" she asked.

"An hour, at three-fifty."

"Should we make one for Daddy?"

"No."

She drummed her fingertips on the storm window. "We didn't forget your birthday, did we?"

"It's not till May."

"If you're still here, Annie and me'll bake you the German chocolate cake with coconut frosting."

I kept my back to the door. "Homemade's better than a bakery cake," Sara went on, parroting her mother, who was adamantly against anything that wasn't made from scratch. I didn't share this dislike, but Charlotte had passed it on to the girls. Little bits of her were always coming out in them. Sometimes this made me want to observe them closely; sometimes, like now, I had to look away.

I waited for the door to close, but it didn't. Like her mother, Sara was stubborn. No matter how hard I braced myself against Charlotte, in the end, I'd do anything for her. Be the hindquarters the Halloween she wanted to dress up as Mr. Ed. Pass secret notes to her boyfriend when she'd been grounded. Go to the racetrack on the hottest day of the year, when all I wanted was to sit by the lake and read.

five

EVEN THOUGH a commuter train ran through the center of it, the town where Charlotte and I had been born and raised was, strictly speaking, a village, and when we were kids, we loved that, because a village sounded like something out of *Jane Eyre*. It was so small that our parents were on a first-name basis with just about all the other adults in the neighborhood.

Now, though, I wished the town was a bigger place. The checkout woman at the market had been my chemistry lab partner, and the bank teller was my Girl Scout leader's youngest son. The intimacy made me uncomfortable, but Annie and Sara were always thrilled to run into someone they knew, even their dentist.

The streets in town seemed more shady than I remembered from childhood; trees and hedges had grown up to hide houses that were once in plain view. The corrugated box factory near the river had burned down a few years back, and in its place was a horseshoe-shaped shopping center with a candy store, pizzeria, and a big man's clothing shop. Annie and Sara haunted that place. They could bicycle there in no time. On Friday night I handed out their allowances, and the next morning, they would set out first thing to spend it.

One Saturday morning in March, I came downstairs as the girls were just getting home. "Did you two have breakfast?" I asked them.

When they shook their heads, I asked, "Will you eat eggs if I make them? I won't bother if no one's going to touch them."

"I'm starving," Sara said.

From the refrigerator, I took a carton of eggs and a stick of butter. "Aunt Lou?" said Annie.

"What?"

"Wanna make a bet?"

"What kind of bet?"

"I bet you a dollar you can't fry an egg without breaking the yolk," she said.

Sara giggled. Already it had become a standing joke between the two of them that I wasn't the world's greatest cook.

"You're on," I said.

I took the cast-iron frying pan from its hook on the wall and set it on the front burner. After dropping a pat of butter in the center of the pan, I turned the flame on low. It was ridiculous for me to be feeling nervous; I'd been frying eggs since I was Sara's age. Holding my breath, I tapped the egg on the edge of the pan. The shell cracked neatly and the insides landed, yolk intact.

"Lucky," Annie said.

The egg sizzled away, but I wasn't done yet. It wouldn't be at all unusual for me to wreck the egg in the process of transferring it from the pan to a plate. But this time, I was painstakingly careful, and when I triumphantly set the plate on the table, the yolk was a yellow bull's eye. Annie glared at it. "Where am I supposed to get a dollar?" she said.

"I just gave you your allowance last night," I said. "It's already gone?"

Annie shrugged.

"I know what happened to her allowance," said Sara.

"You shut up," Annie said.

"That's enough," I told them. "I don't want to know."

"How come you never want to know?" Sara asked.

"Because I don't like bickering and tattling."

"Can I eat the egg?"

"That one's Annie's. I'm making yours now."

"Forget it, I'm not hungry," Annie said, passing the plate to Sara.

"Never mind the money," I told her. "It was a gentleman's bet."

"What's a gentleman's bet?" Sara asked.

"When you don't bet money."

"Oh." She swung her leg, kicking the rung of Annie's chair.

"You wanna die, don't you?" Annie said.

Sara stopped kicking. "What's the point, if you don't bet money?"

"It's the principle," I said. "I was proving I could fry an egg without breaking the yolk, because Annie said I couldn't."

"Oh."

"I bought the glue to fix the handle of your bike, by the way."

"You need a special glue," Sara said.

"This *is* special," I said, rummaging in the hardware drawer. "Look. 'For tires and other hard rubber repairs.'"

Sam came in and Sara jumped up. "We brought you this," she said, handing him the newspaper.

"Thanks," Sam said.

"Do you want an egg?" Annie asked. "I can fix you an egg."

"I can fix an egg, too," said Sara.

"Just toast," Sam said.

I poured him a cup of coffee. "Daddy?" said Sara.

"What, sugar?"

"Do you want a glass of orange juice?"

"No, thanks."

"Grapefruit?"

"Hmmm?" He turned the page, then folded the newspaper in half.

"I could mix grapefruit and orange together," she offered.

"No, thanks."

"Why do they call it grapefruit?" Sara asked. "It's nothing like a grape."

No one answered. She held on to the counter with one hand and raised her leg in an arabesque. "Daddy, look!"

Sam glanced up. He used to have a way of raising his chin and keeping his eyes focused slightly above his normal eye level. It made him seem eager, as if he were expecting something. Now his neck curved forward, and his hair, with no Charlotte to tousle it every time she came close, waved back perfectly from his forehead.

"Daddy? Isn't this good? Aren't I good?" Sara cried, her leg shaking.

"Very good," said Sam.

"Daddy wants to read his paper in peace," Annie said. She lay a plate of toast in front of him, cut neatly into squares.

Sara bounded over and snatched one. Annie slapped her wrist. "Fat!"

"I am not!"

Annie sat down beside Sam. "I want to sit next to Daddy," Sara shouted.

Still reading the paper, Sam stood up and walked into the living room. "See?" Annie said to Sara. "You spoiled his breakfast."

"I did not!"

"You spoil everything," Annie went on.

"Sara, take this and ask your father to fix your bike," I said, handing her the tube of glue.

Sara hesitated, eyeing Annie, who was sipping Sam's left-over coffee. "Annie bought cigarettes with her allowance," she cried, and ran out of the room.

I turned to Annie. "You could make things easier, you know."

"I could do a lot of things," she said. "I could slit my wrists like the boy in *Ordinary People*."

I picked up a dish towel, but I hadn't washed the dishes yet, so I just stood there clutching it. When I looked back at Annie, she'd taken a cookbook from the shelf behind the table and begun flipping through it.

"We could bake bread," I said quietly.

Annie shook her head.

"What about a devil's food cake?"

"No."

I wiped the counter, then I stopped and looked over at her again. "I could do a lot of things, too," I said.

In a little while, Sara came back in. "I don't think Daddy's going to fix my bike."

"He has things on his mind," I told her.

I was trying to think of a better excuse for Sam when Nan Gordon slipped between the rhododendron bushes that separated our yard from hers. Over the years, she and Charlotte had worn a path. "It's Madame!" Sara cried, and flew to open the door.

"Bonjour, mesdemoiselles," called Nan. The girls curtsied, dropping their heads, their arms wide as if they were holding out full skirts. "Très bien," said Nan. "Louise, I'm all out of flour. Can you spare a cup?"

"Sure."

"What're you making?" Annie asked.

"Strawberry tarts," said Nan. "They had strawberries from California at the market today. That means winter's really over."

"Madame Gordon, look!" Sara was trying her arabesque again.

"Hold your stomach in," said Annie. "Madame Gordon, can I come help you bake?"

"If your aunt says it's all right," Nan said.

Sara let her leg fall. "Can we? Can we?"

While the girls were finding their jackets, Nan said quietly, "This'll give you a break."

I wanted to ask her what I was supposed to do while the girls were at her place. The house was spotless, and I'd already spoken to my mother down in Florida. Even she was running out of topics for us to discuss.

Charlotte had always managed to keep busy. When she first moved back to town, she volunteered for everything. She went ballroom dancing one afternoon a week at the senior citizens' home. For a few years, she ran the annual toy and clothing drive at the elementary school, and on Thanksgiving, there were always extras at her table, people with no place else to go. But eventually, Charlotte seemed to lose interest in those things. She devoted herself to her garden.

I stared out the window. There were things I probably should be doing to the flower beds. They were still covered with mulch and hay. Months ago, seed catalogues had arrived with warnings to get orders in early. I'd glanced at them, wondering what I was supposed to order. It was clearly no simple thing to plant a garden. "There is no cure for crown rot," one catalogue said, and another advised, "Beware of white fly spray which will inhibit plant growth."

There were pages of tools — border spades and border forks, hedge shears and edging shears and lopping shears, Dutch hooks and trowels. Eventually, I'd shut the catalogues away in the hall closet with the rest of Charlotte's mail. I hadn't gotten around to making it stop coming yet.

After the girls went next door with Nan, I walked through the dining room, tiptoed past the study, where I could see Sam sitting at his desk, and climbed the stairs. I paused in front of my room, then continued down the hall.

The master bedroom was musty already, like a room in a historic house. I sat down on the bed and peered into Charlotte's night table drawer. In it were half a pack of lemon-honey throat lozenges, a gold chain with a broken clasp, an unopened box of lavender-scented stationery. Everything of Charlotte's had a scent — rose, patchouli, mint. Her toothpaste tasted like licorice.

The drawer was littered with dozens of slips of paper

headed "From the Desk of Charlotte P. Asher." I read the lists like poetry.

Tomato paste, toilet paper, Oil of Olay.

Candles, cherry tomatoes, paper plates, Off.

Razor blades, tarragon, milk.

In the back of the drawer, beneath all the lists, was a foil packet of marijuana and rolling papers. I rolled a joint, found a match in the clutter, and leaned back. I'd done this before. I knew exactly how much pleasure and how much pain to expect at breathing the scent of Charlotte on her pillow.

"You can smell that all over the house," Sam said a little while later, looming above my head.

I hadn't even heard the door open. "The girls are at Nan's," I told Sam.

He took the joint from me, inhaled deeply, then coughed. "Where'd you get this?"

I pointed to Charlotte's drawer.

"The last of her homegrown," he said, sitting down on the edge of the bed.

I watched Sam looking around the room. Charlotte had picked up the mahogany bedroom set for next to nothing at an antiques barn upstate. She'd nursed both babies in the rocker. There was a name for the pattern of the lace she'd made the curtains with — Rose of Sharon or Lilies in the Field, I couldn't remember which.

"Do you think Annie and Sara would like gerbils?" Sam said, after we'd been silent for what seemed a long time.

"Gerbils?"

"A guy in the office just bought his kids gerbils."

"Gerbils are like mice, right? Or am I thinking of hamsters?"

"Hamsters are the furry ones, I think. Like guinea pigs. Maybe they'd like guinea pigs better."

"I once had a friend who had a guinea pig," I said.

"I couldn't have hamsters because we had a dog."

"I'd rather have a dog than a hamster."

"I guess I could get the girls a dog," Sam said.

"I guess." The last thing I wanted was something else to take care of.

The joint had gone out in Sam's fingers. "But maybe Annie would rather have a computer," he said.

"She's always talking about wanting one."

"I guess I better think about it," Sam said. "Gerbils or a computer."

We sat there a little longer, then he asked me, "Where's Richard now?"

"Probably still in bed," I said. "Probably reading a week's worth of newspapers and drinking a pot of coffee. We never used to get going on Saturdays till the middle of the afternoon."

I stood up and went over to the window. It was pretty clear that Richard wasn't going to make a special trip east to come visit me. He thought moving out here was a terrible idea — worse than colorizing old movies.

"Remember the Christmas we went shopping together for Charlotte and Richard?" Sam said. "When we found the turquoise vase? You were in love with Richard, and Charlotte and I had been together forever, so I let you have it, and I went out the next day and bought her a cashmere sweater. But I was always sorry. Charlotte would have loved that vase."

How could I not remember? The vase was Venetian glass, and Sam and I had spotted it in the window of a gift shop in Greenwich Village. On Christmas Eve, just as Richard opened the box and lifted the vase out of the tissue paper, his cat sprang onto the arm of his chair, and too fast for either Richard or I to try and rescue it, the vase seemed to leap out of his hands and smashed to bits on the hardwood floor.

ſix

A WEEK before we were to leave for Florida, where we were spending Easter vacation, Sam asked me to do him a favor and take the girls away without him. Although I would have liked to ask him the same thing, he claimed he was swamped at work, so I agreed.

When Annie and Sara and I stepped off the plane, it was drizzling, and by the time we collected our luggage, it was pouring. My father was waiting out front. After kissing us, he opened a striped golf umbrella, and huddling beneath it, we made our way through the puddles to the car.

Once inside, my father turned to the girls and said, "I'm taking you to the mall tomorrow and buying you sweatshirts," he said.

"We brought sweatshirts with us," Annie told him.

"Not new ones that say 'Florida,'" he said, mopping the rain from his face with a hanky.

Sara said, "I hate Florida."

"That's not true," I said. "On the plane you could hardly wait to get here."

"I'm freezing," she whined.

Annie clamped her hand to Sara's forehead. "I hope you're not coming down with something."

Getting into the car, I caught my father's eye and winked, but he didn't wink back. The hibiscus bushes that lined the road were shivering. "He's no better," my mother had told me the last time we talked. She said she was glad that the girls and I were coming down, for the company and because it meant her stay in Florida was almost over. She and my father would be flying home with us.

"If it doesn't clear up, we can go visit the Indian reservation and see the alligator wrestling," my mother said at supper that night, passing around the platter of fried shrimp a second time.

"Real alligators wrestling?" Sara asked, perking up.

"A man wrestles an alligator, dummy," said Annie.

"They give those alligators drugs," I said.

"Oh, honey, drugs?" said my mother. "I don't think they give them drugs."

"When it rains in Florida, people will do anything," my father announced.

"Now, that's true, Phil," my mother said. "That's very true." She looked pleased that he'd spoken; she'd have agreed with whatever came out of his mouth.

Sara tapped my elbow. "We're supposed to call Daddy."

"He's probably not home yet," I said.

"We could call him at the office."

"You talk to Sam," my mother told my father. "Find out why he's not down here."

When we were alone, my mother lay her hand over mine. "You're doing something to your hair," she said.

"It was looking mousy."

"Sam should have brought the girls. You need a rest." She lowered her voice. "Did I tell you I met a woman at the pool who goes to a spiritualist in Miami? She lost her husband a year ago. She says she's positive she hears him."

"It's all special effects," I said. "Power of suggestion."

"How can you be so sure?"

"They just want your money."

"Strange things happen all the time," my mother said. "One afternoon, I was sitting right there, on that chair, and the door opened and it was Charlotte. I wasn't surprised. It wasn't a dream. It was as if I was expecting her."

"I know what you mean," I said. "I was in her closet once when the girls were at school. She grabbed my shoulder." I demonstrated, my palm landing on my mother's shoulder, then tightening until the fabric of her sweatshirt was balled up in my fist. I did it gently, not like Charlotte, who used to lift my shoulder practically out of its socket. I didn't need a spiritualist to tell me who it was. Charlotte grabbed hold of me that way when she caught me about to borrow something.

My mother frowned. "Charlotte was always happy to lend you her things," she said. "But she wanted you to ask. You never asked."

"She didn't ask either."

"I don't want to hear it." My mother reached for Sara's plate and scraped the leftovers onto hers, then reached for mine.

I glanced around. Everything in the place was new. The floors were covered with pale, bouncy wall-to-wall carpeting. The coffee table was a sheet of glass balanced across a chunk of marble. On the walls here were tasteful beach landscapes. I wondered if my parents missed the multicolored afghans that hung over the backs of chairs at home, or the vinyl apple-shaped placemats. But I thought I understood. Surrounded by brand-new things, my parents could pretend that they were starting out all over again.

"Your father's agreed to go see someone," my mother said.

"Who?" I asked.

"A psychiatrist," she said. "He's going to give it a try when we get home."

"A Jungian or a Freudian?"

"Whoever Dr. Finch recommends. They're not getting into any of that. They're just going to talk."

"I can tell Daddy what his problem is," I said. "He's never been able to cope with trouble. You wouldn't even let Charlotte and me argue in front of him."

"Your father had a very high pressure job. I didn't feel he

should have to come home to screaming and shouting. I wanted him to be able to relax in his own home. Besides, he's not hard-boiled like the rest of us."

"You sheltered him," I said. "That's why he can't handle anything."

My mother sighed. "When you were a baby, he used to sit with you on his lap and sing lullabies. I'd come in and you'd be wide-awake, watching him sleep."

I'd heard this a hundred times. "What conclusion am I supposed to draw from that?" I asked.

"Blame me," my mother said. "If it makes you feel better."

"Remember how he tried to separate Charlotte and me?" I said. "He never understood one thing about us."

"Why should the two of you be on top of each other when we have a big enough house that you can each have your own room?" my father had reasoned. "We'll fix up the back room however you like. It even has a TV."

He'd come home early from work, in time to see me escape from the backyard log cabin in which Charlotte had imprisoned me and go after her with a long stick. The next morning, he told us we couldn't share a bedroom anymore. One of us would have to move into the maid's quarters, a cold little room over the garage.

"This was my room first," Charlotte insisted. "If anyone moves, it's not going to be me."

"The back room has its own bathroom," my father said. "No more arguments over toothpaste or who's taking too long in the tub."

Later, after I'd refused to move, I heard my mother say, "It's normal, Phil. They're so close in age. When they're not fighting, they're best friends."

Even though she was an only child, my mother understood about Charlotte and me because of the way her father was with his sister. "You have a solid foundation," she'd say, as if we were an office building, and I would imagine Charlotte on the forty-second floor and me on the twenty-sixth, or Charlotte on the sixteenth and me on the thirty-seventh, always listening for each other, trying to hear through empty corridors to where the other was.

In Florida, Annie and Sara shared the second bedroom, and I slept on the pullout couch. The first few mornings, I woke to see my father on the balcony, shaking his head. The weather vane was going crazy in the wind. A polished wooden fish with thin copper wings which Charlotte had made in summer camp, it was, I realized, the only knickknack that my parents had brought from home.

In the rain we visited the Indian reservation, the Seaquarium, and an orange grove, my mother worrying the whole time that the girls would catch cold going around in soggy sweatshirts and sneakers. During supper, my parents would watch the news to find out the weather at home. Knowing it was raining there, too, gave them some consolation.

After the weather report, my father played solitaire, the girls watching over his shoulders. "Red queen," Sara said, one evening.

"Hmmm?" he said.

"Red queen. Over there."

He moved the card.

"Two of hearts, Grandpa." Annie pointed.

"Right," he said.

Finally he found another pack of cards for them. They played fifty-two pickup until my mother lost her temper. "Play old maid," she said. "Play war."

"I don't want to," Sara whined.

"Then read a book."

"I hate Florida," Sara said.

"Then go home," said my mother.

It was still raining the next day, and after lunch I escaped to the bathroom and filled the tub with bubble bath. But I had forgotten to lock the door, and just as I was starting to relax, Sara invited herself in. "You're getting pruny," she told me.

"This is what it's like getting old," I said, holding up my wrinkled fingertips.

"Aren't you ever going to get married?"

"You sound like Grandma."

"Well?" Sara said.

"Well, what?" said my mother, coming in and straightening the bathroom rug with her toe.

"I was asking Aunt Lou when she's going to get married," Sara said.

"Good question," said my mother.

"What about Mrs. Martin's son?" Sara suggested.

"Now there's a possibility." My mother knelt down, picked up a washcloth, and started scrubbing my back.

"He's really hunky," Sara told me. "We met him in the elevator. He carried Grandma's groceries."

"He seems very friendly," my mother said, squeezing the washcloth over my shoulder blades.

"His shoulders are out to here," said Sara, holding her arms straight out. "I bet he's a jock."

"Who?" said Annie, coming in.

"You can't tell a book by its cover," my mother said to me. "Just because he has big shoulders doesn't mean he has no brains."

"I've got nothing against big shoulders," Annie said, leaning over the sink with my mascara wand.

"Put that down," said my mother. "I'm talking to Aunt Lou."

"Aunt Lou already has a boyfriend," Annie said.

"She does?" said Sara.

They all looked at me. I folded my arms across my chest.

"Richard," said Annie.

"Why, of course," my mother said.

"But he never even calls," said Sara.

"Yes, he does," Annie told her. "After everyone's in bed,

then he calls." She leaned over and tapped my shoulder. "It's my turn."

"Leave Aunt Lou alone," my mother said. "There's another bathroom."

"But Grandpa's in there, playing cards," said Annie.

My mother dropped the washcloth into the soapy water, and hurried out of the room.

"Is something wrong with Grandpa?" Sara said.

"He's suffering," I said.

"But isn't he supposed to try and hide it from us kids?"

Later that afternoon, when the rain finally let up, the girls and I took a walk on the beach. We kept our eyes peeled. "You never know what you'll find after a storm," I told them.

Sara examined a scrap of faded plastic, then tossed it. "Look," she said, nudging a jellyfish with the toe of her sneaker.

"Don't touch," I said. "It can sting."

"I know that," she said. With a stick of driftwood, she gently batted the jellyfish toward the water, but every time she managed to land it in the ocean, a wave drove it back to shore. Methodically, Sara kept at it until I couldn't bear to watch anymore. I grabbed the stick from her, lifted the jellyfish into the air, and hurled it past the breaking waves.

"Murderer!" Sara screamed.

"It was already dead."

"How do you know? Anyway, it was mine."

"Come on. We'll find another one," I promised, but Sara sulked all the way back to the house.

It seemed as if one or the other of the girls was always sulking. Hard as I tried, I still made mistakes. Certain things, they were too shy or too polite to tell me — that Charlotte had always come into the dressing room when they were trying on new clothes, for instance. And that I'd done the Christmas tree all wrong. I'd invited my parents over for shortbread and hot chocolate, and we had trimmed it together. Later Annie let me know that Charlotte used to do it all by herself and surprise them. She and Sara would walk in after an ordinary day at school, and the tree would be up, lighted, twinkling.

When I first moved in, I stood in the back of the auditorium at PTA meetings. I forgot to say "Asher residence" when I picked up the phone. I kept the radio on during dinner until Sam reminded me that Charlotte had insisted on conversation during meals, no TV or music. When Annie was suspended for smoking in the bathroom at school, I taught her to knit and made her give the scarf to her teacher. When the dentist said there was a possibility that Sara might need braces, I told Annie I'd fine her a dollar if she ever made fun. I hoped that, after a while, I wouldn't have to try quite so hard. Maybe I was starting to catch on.

That night, my mother wanted to go out to dinner for a change, and my father drove us to a restaurant set on stilts directly above the Intracoastal Waterway. From our table by the window, we could see a man in a grimy butcher's apron gutting fish while a pelican dove for the heads. My father couldn't take his eyes off the man.

"Phil's dying to go fishing," my mother whispered to me. "But he won't go alone." Without Charlotte, there was no one to take daylong fishing trips with him. Just setting foot on a boat made the rest of us queasy.

After dinner, the girls played tic-tac-toe on the waxed paper tablecloth, and my father excused himself. My mother swiveled in her seat to watch, until he disappeared through a swinging door. Then she sighed, and crumpled her napkin into a ball.

When my father returned, he was followed by Mrs. Martin, my parents' neighbor, and a tall, blond guy who I figured was her son. "Look who I found," my father said, fitting a chair for Mrs. Martin between himself and my mother.

"Lou, this is Steven," my mother said.

"Steven, the Posts are opposite me on the Intracoastal side," said Mrs. Martin. "The sunsets there are absolutely gorgeous."

"Oh, but Rita, you have the ocean view," my mother said.

Annie held her hand out to Steven. "I'm Annie," she said.

"Steven, Lou teaches music," Mrs. Martin said.

"What do you do?" Annie asked Steven.

"Sales," he said. "Computers."

"I want my dad to buy us a computer," Annie said.

"The girls love those games like Popcorn," I told Steven.

Annie shook her head. "I liked that maybe two years ago."

Sara tapped Steven's arm. "Do you eat your skin when it peels?"

He laughed. "I used to."

"That's disgusting," Annie said.

"Why?" said Sara. "It's just skin."

"It's cannibalistic," said Annie.

"You play tennis?" Steven asked me.

I shook my head. "Not very well."

"She has an excellent backhand," my mother said.

"Charlotte could serve 'em," said my father. "A tennis ball was bald when she got through with it."

"More coffee?" said the waitress, holding the pot above my father's cup.

"Yes, please," he said.

"Charlotte's my mother," Sara told Steven.

After that, everyone was quiet. I found myself watching Steven out of the corner of my eye. The easy way he had with the girls reminded me of Richard. But Richard would never be caught sitting quietly. Richard talked as if his life depended on it. He talked as he brushed his teeth, spraying white on the bathroom mirror. He talked in his sleep. He talked in my sleep, still.

"Was that you in the pool this afternoon?" Annie asked Steven.

He nodded.

"You're fast," she said.

"Sometimes I go into a kind of trance when I swim," he told her.

"Like a zombie?" asked Sara.

Steven laughed. "Sort of."

"A zombie is a dead person, like my mom," said Sara.

I quickly yanked Sara out of her chair and hustled her outside. Together we walked to the end of the pier and looked back. From there, the restaurant was just a tiny, lighted box. "Is she really never coming back?" Sara asked me.

Annie would have said it was a silly question, but I knew what Sara meant. Every time the door opened, we all held our breath. If a stranger referred to the girls as my daughters, Sara and Annie whirled around, looking to see who was standing behind them.

Sometimes I could actually feel Charlotte watching me. I couldn't tell, though, if she was looking on with approval or anger. How would I feel if she was teaching my piano students, rearranging my apartment, conducting my glee club? At the beginning, I'd been certain I was right to take her place, but maybe it was Richard who was right.

The day we were all going home, Sara counted only four suitcases waiting by the door. "One's missing," she told me.

"Go ask Grandma."

While Sara ran off to my parents' bedroom, I went into the bathroom to make sure I'd remembered to pack our toothbrushes and to look in the mirror one more time. I hardly recognized myself, the color of toast. The whites of my eyes gleamed.

Sara ran in. "They have the door closed, and Grandma's yelling again," she reported.

I found my wallet on the kitchen counter and handed Sara all my change. "Run down to the candy machine," I told her. "Buy some gum for the plane. We'll meet you in the lobby. Where's Annie?"

"Playing shuffleboard with Steven," Sara said. "I'll go get her."

After Sara left, I examined the row of bags and saw that it was my father's blue canvas case that was missing. I waited as long as I could, then knocked on my parents' door. "If we don't leave now, we won't make the plane," I called. In a moment, my father appeared, closing the door behind him. He was still in swim trunks and a polo shirt. "Your mom will be ready in a jiffy," he said. He reached over and touched my hair. "You look so pretty, tan."

When I pulled away, he looked stricken. My mother had always thought him brave because his business was coping with fire. When he used to be wakened in the middle of the night, she'd say, "My poor hero." But once he was appointed commissioner, he didn't have to go near the burning buildings. My father had probably forgotten everything he ever knew about putting out flames.

The bedroom door opened again and my mother came out in the high-heeled sandals she usually left in Florida. Once we got off the plane in New York, the sandals were going to look silly, but for now, they helped my mother make her point. Silently, my father and I watched her teeter down the hall. At the front door, she turned. "Lou, let's get a move on."

Not looking at my father again and not bothering to check the dresser drawers and beneath the beds one last time, I went after her. As we bent to pick up the suitcases, my father hurried over. "Let me give you a hand," he said.

"We don't need a hand," my mother said.

Waiting for the elevator, she kept looking back at the apartment door. But once she'd slammed it behind us, the door stayed shut. More sad now than angry, my mother turned to me. "Only your father could work it so it looks like I'm leaving him," she said.

ſeveN

NOT LONG after the girls and I came home from Florida, I was summoned for a conference by Annie's math teacher, Mrs. Green. Approaching the junior high that spring day, I passed the liquor store where Charlotte and I used to buy wine with fake IDs and the park whose shrubs had sheltered us as we drank. I passed the stream we'd crept along to the hollow, where the smoke of our cigarettes wouldn't waft toward school and betray us.

I found my way to the classroom easily; with my eyes closed, I could have found it. In that same room, Mrs. Green had taught first Charlotte and then me, years ago.

When Mrs. Green saw me, she gave me a kiss. I was wondering how it was possible that she looked the same as ever, when she said, "Louise Post, you haven't changed a bit."

She waved away a boy standing by her desk. "To the principal's office," she commanded him. "Ask Mr. Marvel what he thinks of homework written on the centerfold of *Playboy*."

I giggled, and the kid smirked. Mrs Green eyed us both sternly. After he'd left the room, she took a folder from her desk. "I wasn't going to say anything," she said, opening it. "I think of Charlotte and I think of your dear parents, but then I look into Ann Louise's eyes, and I know that unless she deserves it, it would be wrong of me to pass her." She held Annie's math quizzes out in a fan, each one topped with a red letter.

After I'd glanced at them, Mrs. Green laid the papers down

and juggled a bit of chalk. "Annie is just like you, Louise," she said. "A smart girl with no aptitude for math."

Mrs. Green had used those same words to describe me once before, when I failed a math test. That time, I couldn't keep the tears from welling up in my eyes, and she'd bustled me out of the classroom and around the corner to the teachers' lounge, where kids were ordinarily forbidden to go. She'd sat me down on a black vinyl couch and handed me the handkerchief that hung folded from the belt of her print dress and smelled of stale orange blossoms. "Charlotte gets all A's," I'd sobbed.

"You're two different people," Mrs. Green had reminded me, but I refused to believe that.

"How many square yards of linoleum are needed to cover a kitchen floor that measures seventeen and a half feet by twenty-two?" Mrs. Green would ask. She taught math with practical applications always in mind. She insisted that mathematics was no mystery but a science — the science of number, quantity, and space.

But what fascinated Charlotte was the mysterious side — imaginary, irrational, and infinite numbers. There, I was totally lost. I couldn't understand how something as simple as one third could also be expressed 0.3333, threes going on forever. It was beyond logic, as far as I was concerned. It contradicted what you saw in front of you — a cake that could easily be divided into three pieces with nothing left over. Only when you tried to express it in numbers did you run into trouble.

"Get Charlotte to help you," Mrs. Green had suggested more than once.

Charlotte tried, just as hard as she'd tried to teach me to apply eyeliner. We sat in the basement at a miniature chalkboard we'd used when we were little kids. "No, dummy!" she cried. "To get the circumference of a circle, you've got to multiply by pi!"

"What exactly is pi?" I asked, trying to sound curious, not desperate, but Charlotte's face went all red and her mouth gaped as if she were about to bite my head off. She was a terrifying teacher.

"You two are never to discuss math again!" my mother had declared, the day she opened the basement door and heard me bawling.

Now Mrs. Green was suggesting I tutor Annie and help her prepare for her final exam. "What she's really looking for is attention. And you probably miss teaching, don't you, Louise?"

Though reluctant, I agreed to help Annie, then I quickly changed the subject, asking how Mr. Green was. I was ashamed to admit that I didn't miss teaching, didn't long for the smell of chalk, the sound of united, off-key voices, or the thud of the drum. I didn't miss the snickers that broke out when my back was turned. I'd promised to give the principal of my school a definite return date by the beginning of the summer, or else he'd be free to hire my substitute for once and for all.

As soon as Annie came home that afternoon, she slunk up the stairs. "What do you want?" she asked when I followed her.

I sat down on Sara's bed. "If you want to talk about math, there's nothing to talk about," Annie said. "Mrs. Green is tougher on me than on anybody else and it's not fair. Just because Mom was good at math, she thinks I should be. It's not fair. Joanne Parker got almost the same grades as me, and she passed. I don't know why I couldn't have had Miss Furman for math. They shouldn't let old people teach. Once they reach forty or something, they shouldn't be allowed." When I didn't say anything, she went on. "What good is math, anyway? I'm going to be a vet. I'm getting an A in science. Did she tell you that? I bet she didn't." Annie slumped down on her bed.

I thought a minute. "What do you imagine it's like, to be good at math?" I finally said.

"Huh?" said Annie.

"I mean, do you think those people see things differently? Do you think we're missing something?"

"Look, I just want to make it to eighth grade," Annie said. "I don't care what I'm missing."

"Take your mother — do you think she saw angles everywhere? Do you think when she looked at the stars, she was figuring how far away they were? Did she know how much her groceries were going to cost before the checkout person added them up? Could she guess your weight to the pound? Could she tell how long the shampoo was going to last?"

I would have gone on longer, but no one was listening. While I'd been talking, Annie had gotten up and left the room.

For the next few weeks, I spent practically every afternoon with Annie and her math, but as the day of the exam drew near, I had my doubts about whether we were making any progress. Even with the teachers' manual that Mrs. Green had lent me, I wasn't much good at problem solving.

"But why?" Annie would ask me. "Why?" No matter how hard I tried, my explanations were never satisfactory.

More and more often our tutoring sessions were winding up as fights, and finally, I gave up. "You're on your own," I told Annie, and the next afternoon, instead of sitting down with her at the kitchen table, I set out with Sara to surprise my mother and take her into town for ice cream.

We found my mother resting on her front porch in her cleaning uniform, an old button-down shirt of my father's and a denim skirt. "It is positively astonishing how filthy a house can get with only one person living in it," she said, fanning her face with a leaflet that had arrived in the mail.

"You need a sundae," I said.

"I can't go like this." She tucked a stray hair back into her bun.

"You look fine."

"I'll change. Sara, come help me pick out a dress."

Sara kicked the step. "Aunt Lou can help you."

My mother raised an eyebrow. "She's upset that I've been spending all my time with Annie," I explained as we climbed the front stairs in my mother's house.

"Oh, coming here is the booby prize, is that it?"

I laughed. "What Sara doesn't understand is she's better off doing her homework on her own. Me teaching Annie math is like the blind leading the blind."

"Math never was your subject, was it?" said my mother, opening her closet door.

"Wear that," I said, pointing to a turquoise shirtwaist. "That color's beautiful on you."

She held the dress by the hanger up against her. "I hope it's not too tight," she said. "Everything suddenly feels tight. I don't know why — I haven't gained. I hate when under the arm is tight. Do you think I've gained?"

I shook my head and watched my mother take off her skirt and blouse. "Do I look like I've gained?" she asked, turning to me in her slip.

"Mom?"

"What?"

"Do you think it's too late to make plans to send the girls away to camp?"

She looked closely at me, but before she could answer, the screen slammed downstairs and Sara screamed, "A cat got me!"

My mother tossed the dress on the bed and headed for the door. "What next?"

"I'll take care of it," I said quickly, ashamed of what I'd just said.

"He didn't need to scratch me," Sara said, as I led her into the kitchen. "I was just talking to him. I wasn't going to hurt him or anything."

Her arm had puffed up around the red scratch, and I wrapped a few ice cubes in a dish towel and held them against her swollen skin. "What were you talking to the cat about?"

"None of your business," Sara said.

"That's not very polite," I told her.

"But it's the truth," she said.

Charlotte hadn't believed in politeness for its own sake, and she'd encouraged Annie and Sara to express their feelings. "Just look at how you and I act in restaurants," she once said to me. "You wouldn't send that salad back the other day and anyone could see the lettuce was three days old."

Sara stared at her wounded arm. "It's bad, isn't it?"

"Brave girl," I said. When she relaxed against me, I held her close. Maybe I didn't touch Annie and Sara enough. I waited for them to come to me, because I never knew when they were going to shove me away.

"I didn't mean to make the cat mad," Sara whispered.

"It's a cat's instinct to scratch," I told her.

"Why?" she said.

I let go of Sara. I'd had enough of questions.

"Everything okay?" my mother called, appearing in the kitchen doorway. She wasn't wearing the turquoise dress after all. She bent and kissed Sara's cheek. "That's from your grandfather." Then she came over and kissed me.

"You talked to Dad?"

She nodded, as if it was no big deal.

I was relieved to hear that the two of them were in communication. I'd been worrying about my father down in Florida alone. He wasn't young. He could have a heart attack swimming in the ocean with no one to watch him. It wasn't so farfetched a possibility that he could be eaten by sharks in those warm waters. His cholesterol was too high; he pushed himself; he needed to be reminded to take his heart medicine. What if he slipped in the shower? He could easily slip in the shower, break his leg, and lie for days in agony before anyone would notice he was missing.

"Did Dad say anything?" I asked my mother.

She shook her head.

"What's he doing down there?"

"Roasting, I hope," she said. "Seeing a psychiatrist. He could have seen a psychiatrist up here like we planned." She adjusted the waistband of her skirt. "He says the doctor says it's perfectly normal to need to be alone after a death in the family." She sniffed. "A semiretired psychiatrist from Rochester tells him that, and he listens."

"Well, maybe it'll help," I said.

She shook her head. "What's normal is for families to stick together," she said. "When my mother died, Aunt Clara moved in with Pop till he was on his feet again. What may be normal in Rochester is certainly not normal in my family."

"Where's Rochester?" Sara said. "What's wrong with Rochester?"

My mother picked up a dish towel and wiped the counter, which was already spotless. The linoleum shone. The fixtures on the sink gleamed. The dish drainer held one mug and one spoon. My mother used instant coffee now that my father was gone, and claimed not to notice any difference in the taste.

"What's wrong with Rochester?" Sara repeated.

"Nothing," said my mother. "I was just talking."

On our walk into town, Sara stopped to examine an oily rainbow near the curb. "When your Aunt Lou was little, she thought those were real rainbows," my mother told Sara. "And you know those puddles you see on the road when it's hot out? She didn't believe they were optical illusions. Once she actually made me stop the car and let her out so she could run ahead and get wet. The further she ran, the further away the puddles seemed to be. You should have seen how confused she was."

"That was dumb," Sara said to me.

"It was Charlotte," I said. "Not me."

My mother shook her head. "Don't you remember? We were on our way home from the market. Charlotte was up front, and you were in back with the groceries. Charlotte told you it was like Santa Claus and you got mad. You hated believing Santa Claus wasn't real."

When I still wasn't convinced, she said, "Honestly, Lou. You're as bad as your father, only remembering things the way you want them to be. His big complaint is he's not in any of the family pictures. Well, how could he be? He hardly let me touch the camera. He'd holler, 'No, Liz, no, for heaven's sake! You've got your finger over the —— let me do it!'" She did such an accurate imitation of my father's voice that I had to laugh.

She went on, "You think you were the shy one, but in those very same pictures, you're a ham, making faces."

I started to argue, but soon realized it was a losing battle. My mother was adamant, and later that night, when I flipped through the albums, I saw that she was right. I beamed from every photograph, while Charlotte looked self-conscious, her arm protectively around my shoulders. After examining those pictures, I began to wonder what else I'd gotten wrong.

At the ice cream parlor, a towering man stood in front of us on line. He wasn't fat or even heavyset, but his broad shoulders made him seem immense. The back of his neck was red, and he kept fingering his collar as if it was too tight.

When he ordered a peach and chocolate double scoop cone, Sara said, "Excuse me, mister. Those don't go."

He turned around, and my mother cried out, "Why, Fred Lacey!"

Fred Lacey smiled and bent and kissed my mother's cheek. His mother, Nora, was a good friend of our family's, and he and Charlotte and I had practically grown up together, but I hadn't set eyes on him since he went away to college.

After kissing my mother, he kissed me, too. "I wouldn't have known you, Lou. All grown up."

"This is Sara," I told him.

"Hello, Sara." He shook her hand as if she were an adult.

"Sara's my granddaughter," my mother told Fred.

"Oh, so you're married," Fred said to me.

I shook my head, and my mother added quickly, "One of Charlotte's."

Fred looked down at Sara. "Well, what does go with chocolate?" he asked, and lifted her up so she could see into the bins of ice cream under the glass counter and help him pick another flavor.

"I wonder why he isn't married yet," my mother said after Fred had paid for his ice cream and left. "He's so good-looking, it doesn't make sense."

"Do you think he's good-looking?" I asked her.

"I love those black, Irish eyes."

"Grandma, are you going to start going out on dates?" Sara asked.

Our cones came, and my mother pulled napkins from the dispenser and headed toward a small, round marble table under a ceiling fan. When we were seated, Sara said, "Grandma's boy crazy — like Annie."

"I don't think it's up to little girls to tell anyone, let alone strangers, what flavor ice cream goes with what," my mother said.

"But it's true," Sara said. "Fred was wrong."

"Fred wasn't wrong," said my mother. "It's a matter of opinion. It has to do with each person's individual taste, and I think it's very rude of you to be telling people, especially grown-ups, what kind of ice cream they should eat."

Sara's face was turning red. "But my mom said you can't have a fruit flavor ice cream with chocolate. Chocolate can only go with vanilla or coffee or butter pecan. You can't mix fruit with chocolate, and peach is a fruit."

"That's plain silly," said my mother.

"That's what she said!" Sara cried.

"Well, she was being silly. Now sit down and eat, stop waving that cone around."

Sara's eyes narrowed.

"Sara, honey, your ice cream's melting," I said. I reached for her arm, but she jerked away.

"That's that," said my mother, snatching the cone from Sara's hand.

"I hate you!" Sara hissed.

My mother put the cone in an ashtray, struggling to compose herself. Her face was as red as Sara's. She pushed away her dish, wiped her fingertips on a napkin, dabbed her lips. "Well," she finally said, bending her neck to hide the tears in her eyes, and she laid her cheek on the cool marble surface of the table.

The last time I'd seen my mother break down like that was the morning of Charlotte's funeral. She'd crawled into bed with me, her pajama top damp. That morning she made me cry too.

Later that day, I sat in the den with the girls, while upstairs my parents tried to keep Sam calm. Cars came and went — my grandfather's, a cab with Sam's parents, and in between the florist's van with arrangements of gladioli and roses. I broke off a snapdragon from one of the arrangements and showed Sara how to make it open and close as if it were talking.

"I hate this dress," Annie had said.

"Come sit here," I told her, patting the space on the couch beside me.

"Whose stupid idea was it to get navy blue?"

At the church, a neighbor leaned forward and whispered to the girls, "Your mother would be very proud of you two."

"What for?" Sara asked.

"God is watching, and he's proud of what he sees."

"I hate God," Annie said.

Leaving the church, my parents and Sam had been in front of the girls and me, but outside, a crowd was milling and we were separated. I stood still, gripping Annie's and Sara's hands, searching every which way. It seemed as if the entire town had come to Charlotte's funeral.

"Ouch," said Annie, pulling her hand away.

I gave up looking, and led the girls to the car we'd rented until Charlotte's was repaired.

On the way to the cemetery, Annie rode up front, where she fiddled with the radio. "Only AM?" she said.

"Sorry," I said. "Sara, you're as quiet as a mouse back there. Everything okay?"

When Sara didn't answer, Annie looked over her shoulder at her sister, then turned back without a word. I would have taken a look for myself, but we were there, and I made a sharp left through an iron gate and drove up a steep incline.

The cemetery covered the entire hillside. The three of us stood near the summit, staring down. No one else had arrived.

"Where's that?" Sara said, pointing.

"That's town, sweetheart. See the steeple? That's where we just came from."

"It doesn't look right," she said.

I picked up a leaf and twirled the stem between my fingertips. "That's a pin oak," Annie informed me.

The hearse led a procession of cars up the hill. My father jumped out and ran over to us. "Where were you? You disappeared. We couldn't find you."

"We couldn't find you," I told him.

Someone leaned over and kissed my cheek and shook my father's hand, and Sam came to stand between Annie and Sara. "Phil?" my mother murmured from behind us. "Phil, they want us over there."

My father took her arm and led her away. A neighbor of my parents hugged me sideways and said something, but I wasn't listening. Sticking out from the crowd was a shaggy mane like Richard's.

"Right this way, Lou." One of my father's firemen squeezed my elbow.

In the confusion of bent heads and plaid scarves and the bright fall sky, the long-haired guy vanished, or maybe he'd never been there at all. Maybe I'd made him up, wanting so bad for Richard to have come. I turned around. "There're your folks," the fireman said, pointing.

"Dearly beloved," I heard the priest begin, but then there was a commotion up front, someone saying, "No," someone else saying, "Shhh, honey."

"*No*," the voice cried again, and realizing that it was Sara, I pressed forward toward the grave.

Afterward, Annie said she'd never been so mortified in her entire life, Sara crying like that in front of everybody, even kids from school. Annie had tried to pretend that she wasn't there, while Sara screamed, first that they were not to put her mother under the ground, then wordlessly, a wrenching howl that should have wakened the dead.

eigHt

THE WAY MY MOTHER told the story, she and Nora Lacey had arrived at the hospital within minutes of each other to deliver their first babies. My mother said that Nora gave her courage. "She was in the labor room next to mine, and I never heard a peep. I would've been ashamed to scream when she was being so brave. She was all by herself."

"How did you not scream?" I remember Charlotte asking. "I screamed."

"I screamed inside," my mother said.

"Both times?" Charlotte was skeptical.

"She was easy," my mother said, nodding at me. "You were the wrath of God. You were upside down, then sideways. You fought every inch of the way. You braced yourself. You refused to budge. You kicked me in places I'd never been kicked before."

"And you never screamed? Not once?"

My mother shook her head.

"Is it braver to scream or keep quiet?" I asked.

They both looked at me. "Just wait till it's your turn," Charlotte said.

Sharing a room as they convalesced, Nora and my mother became friends. Three months later, when Nora's husband walked out on her for good, my mother was over at Nora's house every single day. So from the start Charlotte and Fred were thrown together, at play groups and birthday parties and ballroom dancing lessons. They were in the same class at school until Fred received a scholarship to a private academy in town. Charlotte went on to public high school.

From then on, my mother held Fred up to Charlotte as a shining example of what could be accomplished. "Look at Fred, he's going to Harvard. No father — just hard work and perseverance got him there."

And then: "Fred's going to England to study next fall, and Nora's going to visit him at Christmastime. The rate I'm going, I'll never get closer to Europe than a postcard."

And finally: "Nora's flying to Boston for Fred's graduation. How many Ph.D.s do you know?"

"Fred's weird," Charlotte always said, and my mother would glare at her. "Here Fred Senior disappears into thin air one morning, and Fred and Nora have to carry on alone. Where's your sympathy? Where's your human kindness?"

But even my mother couldn't deny that Fred was different. We'd always heard that he was going to enter the priesthood, but for some reason, he became a professor of Western religion instead. "Maybe he wasn't good enough," I said, but Charlotte sniffed. "If anything, he's too good," she told me.

There wasn't a whole lot to say about Fred. Although he never became a priest, he seemed to live like one. I'd never heard a word about a girlfriend. He lived near Boston College, where he taught, and he was writing a book. According to Nora, he'd been working on it for ages and it took up every second of his spare time.

The spring we met Fred at the ice cream parlor, he'd graded his final exams, packed his bags, and moved back home for a year of sabbatical, during which he planned to finish his book. Nora thought he'd come home to breathe some good fresh air, but my mother suspected he'd made the decision on account of Nora's gallbladder giving her trouble lately. The house that Fred was renting for the year was only a block from the apartment Nora had moved to when he'd gone away to school, and not even a five-minute walk from our house.

.   .   .

The girls' summer vacation did not start off with much promise. Day after day, it rained. I couldn't blame them for being cranky, but I was at my wit's end, trying to come up with indoor activities for them.

Then, one afternoon, the bell rang, and when I opened the door, it was Fred. We hadn't spoken since the time at the ice cream parlor, but after all, I'd known him all my life, and pretending to wipe sweat from my brow, I said, "Thank God."

Fred looked confused. "Excuse me?"

I pulled him inside. "What I meant was, we could use some company."

"I happened to look out the window just as the rain stopped, and I decided to go to the diner for a snack," he said. "I wondered if you and the girls would care to join me."

"Definitely," Annie called from the living room, where she and Sara were playing their hundredth game of spit.

At the diner, Fred ordered hot tea and cinnamon toast for all of us without asking and didn't try to get the girls to talk. "How's Len?" he asked the waitress, a redhead named Bonnie, who wore a studded black leather band around her wrist.

"You remember what I told you, what he said?"

Fred nodded.

"Well, after that, Cindy — you know, who used to date him? She said he was just saying that to me to make Marilyn jealous."

Fred slowly ran a finger over his lips. The girls and Bonnie didn't take their eyes off him. "I think more likely he's worrying that you're still thinking about —"

"Don't say it!" Bonnie screeched. "You're crazy to think that word is even in my vocabulary anymore!"

Bonnie brought Fred a piece of pie à la mode, on the house, and asked how his book was coming along. She told Annie she liked her hair and gave Sara an order pad, for keeps. On my way to the ladies' room, she stopped me. "I just want you to know, Lou, that a lot of girls in this town model themselves after your sister," she said.

When I returned to the table, I told the girls we should get going.

"Do we have to?" Sara said.

I nodded. "Annie has some studying to do."

"But it's vacation," said Fred.

"I failed math," Annie explained.

"I'm sorry to hear that."

Annie shrugged. "It's not all my fault. Mrs. Green is unfair, and Aunt Lou was supposed to be helping me."

"Mrs. Green?" Fred said, looking at me. "Not our Mrs. Green."

"The very same," I told him.

"She was something," said Fred. "No *buts* about her."

"What does that mean?" Sara asked.

"She wouldn't listen to any excuses," he explained.

"So anyway, I'm stuck going to summer school," said Annie. Her eyes suddenly brightened. "Are you any good at math?"

Fred shrugged.

"Fred's a genius," I said.

"A genius like Einstein?" cried Sara.

"I could probably help you," Fred said to Annie. "That is, if you like," he added, looking at me.

"I'd be grateful not to ever have to open a math book again," I said.

Walking home from the diner, the girls ran ahead, sure that the sky was clearing. Fred and I strolled along together, side by side. "You seem different than I remember," he said, swinging the umbrella he'd brought along, just in case.

I laughed. "Older."

Fred shook his head. "That's not what I mean."

In front of our house, he stopped. "Do you by any chance like Japanese food? Because a new Japanese restaurant just opened out at the mall. Maybe we could try it some time."

"I'd like that," I said.

"Actually, they're having a grand opening special tonight. Two for one. I saw the ad in the morning paper."

I could feel my neck getting hot.

"So, what about it?" said Fred.

"Sure."

"Sure for tonight?"

I nodded and hurried up the walk.

"Good work, Aunt Lou," Annie said admiringly when I told the girls.

"It's not a date," I said. "Fred just wants to try out this new restaurant."

"I mean it. This is not a date," I repeated later, when Annie insisted I wear a dress, not jeans.

"Put this on." She held out a black sleeveless dress that was much too formal, but I obeyed.

She stood back and surveyed me. "It needs a belt."

I hiked the dress up. "Won't that make it too short?"

She frowned and thought for a second. "I know," she cried, and ran out of the room, down the hall.

Sara was coming up the stairs. "Where you going?" she said, following Annie into the master bedroom.

In there on the dressing table was a blue velvet jewelry box that Charlotte had had since high school. I'd spent hours back then watching her search through it, getting ready for a date. "What do you think?" Charlotte would say, holding up a dangly earring. Some days, she was bossy. "Run get Mom's belt, with the coins like Cleopatra." Other times, she'd drop down on her knees and beg to borrow my suede clogs.

The day of a date, she always fasted, drinking nothing but lemon water. She wore my jeans, which were tighter than hers. When her fingers touched Bobby Randolph's in the popcorn container, an electric shock ran through her entire body, she told me later. When John Rosen took her to the natural history museum, he kissed her behind a display of ichthysaurus bones.

I stood in the doorway while the girls emptied the contents of Charlotte's jewelry box onto the bed: the silver medallion Charlotte used to wear to fancy parties, the garnets she inherited from our grandmother, Mardi Gras beads, plastic lanyards from summer camp, the opera-length pearls she was married in.

"Try these," said Annie, handing me a string of amber, warm, as if someone had just taken it off. Then she put her finger to her lips. "Shhh!" She strained to hear someone below us in the hall. "It's Daddy!" she cried. Sam was home and coming up the stairs. Annie and Sara dove under the bed, giggling.

"What's all this?" Sam said from the doorway.

"I'll pick up later." I moved between him and the bed, to shield him from the jewelry.

When the front doorbell rang, Sam was making a fist around Charlotte's coral necklace. "That's Fred," I said. "We're going out to dinner. I promise I won't be late."

"Fred?"

"I won't be late," I said, and I ran down the stairs and out of the house.

On the way to the restaurant I hardly listened to Fred. I was picturing Sam gathering palmfuls of beads and pouring them back into the velvet box. I was picturing the girls beneath the bed, their bodies limp with laughter and then disappointment. Their father wouldn't know he was supposed to search and find them.

At the restaurant, Fred plied me with raw octopus, shark, and squid — things I ordinarily wouldn't have touched. My throat burned with mustard and horseradish, my eyes watered, my lips tingled. After a while, I couldn't speak or see or even hear very well. "Try this," Fred kept on saying. "Try this."

But as he was holding a shrimp toward my mouth, I came to my senses. I shook my head, wiped my lips, took a sip of water. I couldn't believe it. For the first time in a long while, I'd forgotten everything.

"Tell me about your book," I said.

Fred sat back. "It's about free will in relation to Christian theology. It's an old question, really, but I'm hoping I can shed some new light. I'm discussing it historically first, what different philosophers have had to say — Saint Augustine, Thomas Aquinas, Kant, all the way up to Marx and Freud. See, some people don't believe that there is such a thing as free will. They think our thoughts and acts are completely predetermined, by the environment we're born into, by our given natures —"

"Dessert?" asked the waitress, bringing Fred and me small cups of tea.

"No, thanks," I said, glancing at my watch.

"I've bored you," said Fred.

"No, not at all. But it is getting late."

When Fred parked in front of the house, I was feeling guilty that I hadn't been more attentive about his book or more appreciative that he'd paid for dinner. To make up, I asked him in for coffee.

Inside, Nan Gordon was sitting on the living room couch beside Sam. Sam jumped up. "You're home," he said, sounding relieved, I thought.

"The girls are okay?" I asked.

"They went to bed, no problem. Do you know Nan?" he asked Fred.

"I've seen you around," Fred said, shaking Nan's hand.

Sam pointed to a pear tart on the coffee table. "Look what Nan brought over."

"Today was my baking day. I made an extra," Nan explained.

"It looks lovely," I said, wondering what had provoked this.

Fred laughed. "Food's meant to be eaten, not looked at."

I went into the kitchen for plates and forks and a knife. When I came back, Fred had made himself comfortable in the easy chair and was talking. It was a good thing I'd invited him in, or Sam and Nan and I would probably still have been staring at the tart.

"You two should try this place," Fred was saying. "The service was good, and the sashimi was out of this world."

"I don't know much about Japanese food," Nan said.

"There's a sushi bar around the corner from my office, and I sneak over for lunch once in a while," said Sam.

"If you like sushi, you should definitely try this place," Fred said. "I recommend it, don't you, Lou?"

I nodded, and held the knife out to Nan. She took it from me and began cutting long, slender triangles. I would have been more generous.

"It turned lovely today," Fred said, "after all the rain."

"I don't mind the rain, for the garden's sake," Nan said. "But it must be hard on the kids."

"Sara and Annie have been gambling on old maid and spit," I said.

Fred laughed.

"Annie did very well in class this year," Nan said, holding out dessert plates to the rest of us. "She's quite talented."

"Annie's the graceful one in the family," Sam said.

"Delicious," said Fred, after his first bite. "Nan, where'd your accent come from?"

"My mother was French Canadian. We spoke French at home sometimes."

"This is the best pear tart I've ever tasted," Sam announced.

Nan blushed. "I'm afraid the crust is a little dry. I struggle with my crusts."

Sam shook his head. "It's not at all dry."

"Not at all," said Fred. "But I better have another piece to make sure."

"You're both very gallant," said Nan.

Only Nan would use a word like *gallant*. To me, the crust was fine.

"How about a brandy?" Sam said, jumping up and heading for the liquor cabinet.

"That would be lovely," said Nan.

"Did you grow up in Canada?" Fred asked her.

"Just summers. My family had a bungalow north of Quebec. It was the best time growing up."

"I hated summers when I was young," Fred said. "All I got were sunburns and poison ivy. Remember, Lou?"

I nodded. All summer Fred's mother slathered him with lotions — calamine, zinc oxide, Coppertone. Kids used to make fun of him for that and for the spare tire around his waist. He'd been a roly-poly little boy.

Sam poured brandy into four glasses and passed them around.

"Thanks," said Fred. He took a sip, then went on. "The worst part was going to the pool. I had to take my glasses off when I went in the water, and the whole thing was a blur, splashing and screaming, and the lifeguard blowing his whistle."

"I hated the pool back then, too," I said. "Which is funny because when I was living in the city, I used to go swimming three times a week and no one was forcing me to."

"Lou and Charlotte and I grew up together," Fred told Nan.

"Anyone else need a refill?" said Sam, pouring more brandy into his glass, then holding out the bottle.

"No thanks, I should be going." Fred stood up.

"Me too, I guess," said Nan.

Sam and I walked them to the door.

"You two definitely have to try that restaurant," said Fred.

After calling good night and waving from the front steps, Sam and I went back inside. Sam closed the door; then, without a word of warning, he drove his fist hard into it. The skin over his knuckles burst, and I ran to the bathroom for a towel.

After bandaging Sam, I helped him to the couch. When I patted his back, he didn't pull away. He was starting to tremble, and I put a glass of brandy in his good hand.

"It's all right," I said, the only words I could come up with.

"I know." Sam nodded slowly. "It's perfectly all right for me to be flirting with my wife's best friend."

NiNe

As USUAL, my grandfather invited us to his house for Fourth of July weekend, but when I told the girls, they didn't want to go. "It won't be the same," Sara complained. "All the fun people are gone." She ticked them off on her fingers. "Mommy, Grandpa, Richard."

But we went, anyway. "Pop would be hurt," my mother said.

On the drive to the Berkshires, we had to stop five times while she ran with Sara to the nearest bush. It was my fault. I'd forgotten to give Sara her Dramamine. Each stop proved to be a false alarm, but it had Sam so jumpy that he could hardly keep his eyes on the road. "Now?" he kept saying. "Now?" Sara never felt sick at the rest areas, only on stretches of highway with no shoulder.

When we arrived, Aunt Clara appeared in the front doorway, waving. Before the car came to a full stop, my mother sprang out and ran over to hug her, and the two of them disappeared into the house.

"Isn't Aunt Clara going to show us where to park the car?" Sara said.

"We're the only car," Sam said, pulling beneath the willow. "I'm taking a swim. I'll get the stuff out of the trunk later." He slammed his door.

"Daddy's fed up, thanks to you," Annie said to Sara.

"It's not my fault," Sara said, with a meaningful look at me.

The three of us sat in the car, not moving or saying a word. It was already boiling out. My grandfather's house had been built in a hollow for protection against the winter winds; on a day like this, we'd soon be begging for a breeze. Fortunately, the lake was deep enough that it stayed cool.

"What do you think would happen if we drove home right now without telling anyone?" Sara said. "What would they say?"

"No one would care," Annie guessed.

"They'd care," I said. "They'd worry. They'd feel bad." But I did glance down at the ignition. Sam had taken the key with him.

Then we heard someone crunch along the gravel drive, and Aunt Clara stuck her head in the driver's window. "What's wrong?" she said. "Are your fannies glued to those seats?"

"And how are my great-granddaughters today?" asked my grandfather once we'd joined the others around back.

"They're fine," I told him, when neither of the girls spoke up. Sara and Annie were always tongue-tied with their great-grandfather at first.

"I understand you both had excellent report cards," he said to them.

"That's right," I lied, knowing my mother must have told him that.

The girls stared down at their toes, all twenty of them painted pink. My grandfather followed their gaze. "What's that you've got there?" he said, stepping one of his deck shoes forward so that their small feet seemed imperiled.

"Passionate Pink by Revlon," Annie told him.

"Aren't you too young for nail polish?"

"We know what passion is," she said.

"Pop, you've got a new dock here," Sam called. He was standing on the shoreline, peeling off his shirt.

"That's seasoned wood," said my grandfather. "Won't warp."

The moment he took his eyes off them, the girls were gone.

He peered after their retreating backs, shading his thick eyeglasses. "I suspect you're letting those children get away with murder, Louise," he said. "It's going to show, mark my words. The answer to toe polish should have been flat-out no."

"Oh, hush up, Charles," Aunt Clara called from the thicket behind us, where she was clipping wild roses. "What do you know about child rearing? Your wife raised your child. Any good that's in Liz came from Sylvia."

My grandfather's mouth twitched, but he didn't answer. He walked slowly down to the dock, where he bent to pluck a weed growing between the new boards. Suddenly, he straightened and reached for the small of his back.

"Poor Charles," Aunt Clara said. "Everyone he's ever really liked is gone." She handed me a bunch of flowers and moved to the next bush. "How are you doing, Lou?"

"I'm fine."

"Now, you don't have to say that," she said. "You don't have to hide your pain from me."

"Really, I'm doing fine."

She sighed, filling my arms with more roses. "Control can be a virtue, but I'm afraid one day you're going to boil over. Just last week at my women's group we were discussing the question of self-control. For too many years, women have been expected to be the Rock of Gibraltar."

She handed me a few more stems. "Let's get these in water."

As we started toward the house, she said, "When Liz called and told us about Charlotte, it didn't seem possible. Why, I distinctly remember the day she was born. John and I were watching television when the phone rang. 'I'm a great-aunt,' I told him after I hung up. 'What are you talking about?' he said. He thought I meant a-n-t, not a-u-n-t. We weren't expecting to hear any news for another couple of weeks."

We found my mother at the kitchen table, a movie magazine open in front of her. "Look," she cried. "A full-page story about Richard!"

"I saved that for you," Aunt Clara said, taking the flowers

from me and laying them on the cutting board. "I picked up that magazine at the checkout counter, and I couldn't believe my eyes."

I bent to see, and sure enough, there was Richard, wearing a Hawaiian shirt and sunglasses, looking nothing like the way I remembered him. I'd never even seen him wear sunglasses before. He always said he didn't want to see life tinted. Because of that, there were deep lines on his forehead and crow's feet around his eyes. This photo hid everything I loved about him.

"How is Richard?" Aunt Clara said.

"Fine," I said. "He's been busy with his movie. He's back and forth to Los Angeles all the time now." I gave my mother a quick look so she wouldn't start in about Richard and me. That was all I needed. Like a puppy, once Aunt Clara got hold of something, she didn't let go.

Anyway, what was there to say? I'd called Richard in June on his birthday, and all we talked about was the Brooks Brothers suit his mother had given him. "Where am I ever going to go in a Brooks Brothers suit?" Richard had asked me. He wanted to return it and stock up on shirts and underwear and socks, but I was pretty sure I'd convinced him not to. "After all, she's your mother," I said.

The time we'd spoken before that, we argued about the best cure for the hangover Richard was suffering from. "Aspirin and seltzer," I said, but he insisted that only a truck driver's breakfast — ham and eggs and hash browns — would do the trick.

My mother closed the magazine. "Oh, no, Liz, leave it open to Richard's picture for when Charles comes in," Aunt Clara said. "That'll get his blood running."

"Grandfather didn't like Richard, did he?" I said.

"Oh, now, I wouldn't say that," my mother said.

"Face facts," Aunt Clara interrupted. "Charles isn't even sure if he likes us."

.   .   .

Two canoes were making their way across the lake with Sam and my grandfather at the helms. Their pace was uneven, but my grandfather kept the lead. After all the years that Sam had been coming here, he knew better than to try and pass the old man.

The girls were playing mermaid in the water. They lay on their backs and kicked hard, then flipped into surface dives. My mother, Aunt Clara, and I applauded periodically from our chairs.

"How was the weather in Florida this year?" Aunt Clara asked.

"Perfect, when it wasn't raining," said my mother.

"You had a good time?"

My mother nodded. "Lou met a nice young man when she and the girls were down."

"He was more Annie's friend than mine," I said.

"Annie's going to have Charlotte's way with men," Aunt Clara said. "She's the spitting image of her mother. Why, looking at her and Sara, I can step back twenty years. That could be Charlotte and Lou playing in the water. Lou, re-member the summer Charles let both of you plant a row in the vegetable garden? You planted radishes, and Charlotte had the zucchini. Her plants took over the entire garden, and you were furious. Then a groundhog got in under the chicken wire and ate everything. Charles came out with his shotgun, but Charlotte threw herself in front of him and said, 'You'll have to kill me first.'"

Before Aunt Clara had finished, my mother stood and headed straight for the lake. I could practically hear her heart pounding. Because she'd never learned how to dive properly, she usually waded in, but now she went up on the dock and tried, with an awkward belly flop that must have hurt.

"Would you look at that," Aunt Clara said. "Liz is usually the last one in. I know, I know. I shouldn't have said that about Charlotte. But someone has to make Liz start talking. She'd feel a hundred percent better if she'd get it off her chest. She hasn't said a word to me about Phil, either. I'm her aunt, and I want to help. But how can I when I don't know the facts? And by the way, don't think I don't notice that Richard's not here this year."

I kept my eyes on my mother's head and flapping arms. Watching her swim didn't give me much confidence.

When the men climbed out of the boats a little later, Aunt Clara called, "Nice work, Charles. You beat Sam again."

"Daddy, you don't try," Sara shouted.

My grandfather shook his head. "Idiots," he muttered.

"Oh, Lou, I haven't told you about my trip," Aunt Clara said.

"I didn't know you were taking a trip."

My aunt stretched out her bony legs. Her skin was permanently tanned from all the sunning she'd done in her lifetime. "I'm going down the Amazon," she announced.

"Clara, you are starting to make a damn fool of yourself," said my grandfather.

"At night, we'll camp alongside the river, under the moon," she went on.

"To even be thinking such a thing at your age is a sign of senility," he said.

"What's Aunt Clara up to now?" said my mother, wading out of the water. Not even halfway across, she'd given up and turned back.

"I'm going down the Amazon," Aunt Clara said.

"Sounds thrilling," said my mother, bending and shaking her head.

"And just how do you intend to pay for a trip like that?" asked my grandfather.

"For your information, I'm selling the last of the AT&T Father left me."

"When are you going?" said my mother.

"October. That's springtime in South America. Wait till you see the brochures. Thrilling isn't the word."

"Maybe I'll come with you," said my mother.

"The pair of you!" My grandfather shook his head and marched off.

"Think about it, Liz," Aunt Clara said. "Seriously. I'd love the company."

"I'll do that." My mother stretched out on a lounge chair and closed her eyes. She was breathing heavily from her swim. "Lou, stop staring," she said, her eyes still shut.

After dinner, when the china and crystal were washed and dried and put away, and someone had dragged an armchair out back for my grandfather to sit in, it was time for the fireworks. My grandfather loved fireworks, and every year a neighbor brought him a new batch from South Carolina.

"If there's not enough, we can pull out the ones left over from last year and the year before that," Aunt Clara said, lighting more citronella candles. "It's like an arsenal, that basement."

"Here," called Sara, running to Aunt Clara with a marshmallow hanging soft and charred from a stick.

"Careful running with that," I warned Sara.

"Thanks, darling," said Aunt Clara.

"Grandpa, do you want me to make one for you?" Sara asked.

"That's all I need. That would send my digestive track haywire."

"I think two hamburgers would probably have been enough, don't you, Charles?" Aunt Clara said sweetly.

I sat down beside my grandfather. "Well, what about that father of yours," he said. "Should I get involved?"

"Of course you shouldn't get involved," Aunt Clara said.

"I've heard a thousand times what you think," my grandfather said to her. "I'm trying to get Louise's opinion."

"I think they're going to have to work it out for themselves," I said.

"Nonsense! The man's acting like a fool, and someone has to tell him."

"You're the fool," Aunt Clara said swiftly. "Thinking you can run the world from your own backyard."

My grandfather raised his eyebrows and made a sweeping gesture with his arm. His property was far more than a backyard. The lake alone was several acres, and the hillside to the north belonged to him, as well as the gardens and the woods. "Just remember, Clara," he said. "You're here out of the goodness of my heart."

"One day I won't be," she said. "One day you're going to look around and we're all going to be gone."

The next morning, I was up before anyone. Careful not to waken the others, I went out back and pulled a lawn chair closer to the water. The morning after Charlotte's wedding, I'd gotten up early, too, and circled the lake, picking wildflowers for the breakfast table. But halfway around, I'd tossed my bouquet into a bush. Charlotte was the one who loved flowers.

In the far corner of the lake was a fleet of lily pads. After the ceremony, the best man and I had helped Charlotte and Sam into the canoe, and they paddled off while everyone applauded. When they returned, Charlotte had a pink lily in her hair. On the dock, she whispered, "The baby just moved." At that moment, I believed it would be enough the rest of my life to be Charlotte's sister.

Now Aunt Clara came marching down the hill. "Good morning, Lou," she called.

"Morning."

"Come take a swim."

I shook my head.

"Come on. It'll do you good."

"No, thanks."

"Now, don't be glum."

"I'm not glum."

"What do you call it then, your face this long?" She crinkled up her forehead, imitating me. "Come for a swim," she coaxed.

Still, I shook my head.

"Stubborn." When she threw off her terrycloth robe, she was naked except for a white bathing cap. With a perfect jackknife, she dove off the dock.

I was as malleable as dough, not stubborn at all. If someone said a bed of nails was comfortable, I'd probably have lain down on it. I waited for Aunt Clara to swim back so I could tell her she was wrong. I'd given in on the wallpaper in Charlotte's and my bedroom. I always gave in on the restaurants where we were to have lunch.

Aunt Clara touched the dock, and without pausing for a breath, pushed off with her toes. "Aunt Clara!" I called.

She started back across.

"Aunt Clara!"

She kept going, slapping the water with her palms, as if she were swatting flies. I took off my T-shirt and shorts and dove in after her.

When I caught up, I tapped her shoulder. She stopped, sputtering. "Sorry," I said. "I just wanted to tell you I'm not. I'm not stubborn at all."

She stared at me, blinking beads of water from her eyes. "Who but a stubborn person would swim all the way out here just to tell me that?"

teN

AT THE END of one of our late-night, long-distance conversations, Richard and I made plans to meet. "Dinner at my place," Richard suggested, but I insisted on lunch in neutral territory, a restaurant that neither of us had ever been to before. Richard said he'd be back in New York at the end of July, and we set a date.

The day before our meeting, Annie came with me to the mall to help me pick out something new to wear. Walking through the first shop, I felt like Rip van Winkle. "Are people my age really wearing skirts this short?" I asked.

"Where've you been?" Annie fingered a pink dress. "Polyester," she determined, and moved on.

"I don't want to look like I just crawled out from under a rock."

"That's why you've got me," said Annie.

At the jewelry counter, she took three bangle bracelets from a rack and fit them over my wristbone. "Go like this," she said, waggling her hand. When I obeyed her command, the bangles jingled. "Good," she said. "They make you look carefree. Men like that."

"What do you mean?"

"Men don't like women with problems."

"How would you know?"

She sighed. "From experience." She counted her boyfriends on her fingers. "Isaac never wanted to discuss anything. He'd go, 'Lighten up.' Gus was always playing practical jokes, and all Howie wanted to do was throw a Frisbee."

In the dressing room, she looked me up and down. "You have a good body, Aunt Lou."

I stared at myself in the mirror.

"Sit out back this afternoon," Annie advised me. "Your tan needs work. You can borrow my sun reflector. You want to get Richard back, right?"

I shook my head. "I'm trying to break up with him."

"Oh!" she said. "That's different. Turn around." She examined me all over again, then shook her head.

"What's wrong with it?" I was just getting used to seeing myself in the skimpy sundress Annie had picked out.

"Trust me."

When my mother's car turned into the driveway the next morning, Annie and I were already downstairs. "Da da," Annie said, as if I were her creation.

"You're not wearing that," my mother said.

"Why not?" I asked.

"Shorts are for the backyard or the beach," my mother lectured. "Not for the city. Certainly not for a date."

"Those aren't shorts," Annie said. "They're Bermudas made of linen, with a matching jacket."

My mother folded her arms and stared into space. I knew that look. Annie's arms were folded, too, but she was just a kid. I went upstairs to change.

When I came down again in an old flowered skirt, my mother said, "Why do you have to go today of all days? It's already eighty-six degrees and climbing." But then she snapped her fingers and went rummaging in the hall closet. She came out with the battered straw hat Charlotte used to wear to the beach. I backed away, but my mother insisted. "You won't last five minutes on those hot pavements without some protection."

The straw smelled like coconut oil; the brim cast a shadow over my shoulders. "Lovely," said my mother, standing back and nodding. "Very French."

After dropping me at the train station, my mother was taking the girls to the pool. We all squeezed into her car, a Styrofoam cooler up front beneath my feet; rafts, towels, and beach bags piled in back with the girls.

A few blocks from home, Sara let out a shriek.

"If you don't get that raft away from my leg, I'll pinch you again," Annie said.

"Five more minutes," said my mother. "Then one of you can come up front."

"Aunt Lou, if Richard's still your boyfriend, how come he doesn't come and see you?" Sara asked.

When I didn't answer, she complained, "Aunt Lou's not listening."

"Move over!" said Annie.

When we reached the station, my mother said, "Let me know which train you're catching back."

"Buy me something," Sara shouted.

"Be good," I called, glad to be getting away from all three of them.

The restaurant where I was to meet Richard wasn't far from my old neighborhood. I'd come early on purpose, so I'd have time to stop at my building. I wanted to visit Mrs. Rapetti and figure out what to do with my apartment. I'd already written to my landlord about subletting it. Out of the question, he'd said.

I got off the subway at Fourteenth Street and proceeded down Seventh Avenue, past the jewelry shop whose awning read, WE PIERCE EARS, WITH OR WITHOUT PAIN. When I reached the corner deli, I went in, just to see how the owner acted with me. To my relief, she showed no sign of recognition. That was how you knew you belonged. With strangers, she fussed, trying to be helpful.

I continued on, past the cheese shop where I used to buy real Parmesan and ricotta for Charlotte. "How much was it?" she'd ask when I arrived. I'd tell her the cheese was on me, but every single time, she insisted on paying. She'd scrounge around in her wallet and her coat pockets and her junk drawer, making me feel as if I was robbing her of her last dime.

Without the neighborhood church as a landmark, I might easily have walked past my building. Only when I was directly in front of it could I describe it — a dirty brick tenement, six stories high, with a green door.

I pressed the buzzer for Apartment 3, then stepped back onto the sidewalk and waited. In a minute, Mrs. Rapetti's frizzled head poked out. "Yeah?" she hollered. She couldn't see very far.

"It's Lou."

"Mary, mother of Jesus," she cried, and disappeared.

When I first moved in, Mrs. Rapetti had pounded on the ceiling with a broom handle every time I walked across the floor with my shoes on. It was Vinnie who made his way up the stairs to meet me. Big as a bear, he frightened me at first with his halting phrases and wild smile. But soon, we became friends. "Send Vinnie home," Mrs. Rapetti would holler from the fire escape when she heard us laughing. As the summer went on, though, more often she'd call, "Keep Vinnie while I run out for milk. You need something?"

"Lemme touch you," Mrs. Rapetti said, when I reached her landing. She was still in her wrapper. She poked my arm. "You never called, not a card, nothing. Vinnie thought you forgot him."

"Is he home?"

"It's Wednesday, he's at the center. You want coffee?"

I shook my head. Always fearful of catching a chill, Mrs. Rapetti kept her windows shut, even on the hottest days of summer. "It must be a thousand degrees in here," I said. "How's Vinnie?"

"It's me you should worry about."

"Why? What's wrong?"

"I'm old, that's what's wrong."

"But there's nothing medically wrong?"

"How should I know? I could be dying."

Mrs. Rapetti's apartment was cluttered with statues of saints and elaborate crucifixes. Attached to the walls at the entrance of each room were small ceramic bowls of dusty holy water, into which she absently dipped her finger as she passed from room to room.

"I stopped by once to pick up some clothes," I said. "I knocked on your door, but no one answered."

"I must of thought you were the Con Ed," she said. "You should've called up. How're the girls?"

"Sara's gained some weight."

"Nothing worse than a fat kid," said Mrs. Rapetti. "She a whiner?"

"No."

"I never heard of a fat kid wasn't a whiner. Well, it could be worse. It could be drugs. Why you rubbing that arm, you got a rash?"

"Just a mosquito bite," I said.

"See what happens when you leave the city? So when you coming back?"

"I'm not sure."

"What, you're not sure. What about your job? What're you using for money — peanuts?"

"I was thinking I should give up my apartment."

"You crazy?" she said. "Where you gonna find another place like that, the money you pay?"

"Lerico won't let me sublet."

"Lou," said Mrs. Rapetti, "take my advice. Wait. Don't do nothing you're gonna have regrets about."

I nodded. "How's Vinnie?" I asked again.

"He's fine. He put on weight, too. Why he had to find a job at a pizza parlor, don't ask me. I says to him, 'Vinnie, go on a diet, then you can dance with me.'" She laughed. "My sister came up from Jersey last week. We danced. She says, 'No one in the world fox-trots like you, Carmela.' You sure you don't want coffee?"

I looked at my watch and shook my head.

Mrs. Rapetti stood up, wheezing. "See? Trini Lopez is still on the record player."

She lifted the needle into the first groove. She pulled me up into her arms and held me as tight as a man would. There were places she could go to dance right in the neighborhood — social clubs and church groups — but she refused to dance with strangers. At the end of the song, she did some fancy footwork and spun me like a top.

When I arrived at the restaurant, Richard was chatting with the bartender. His hair needed trimming — I'd always done that for him — but aside from that, he looked normal, nothing like the magazine photograph. He had on jeans and an old T-shirt of mine that said PROPERTY OF THE NEW YORK METS. In his loft were other items of clothing we'd shared: a navy flannel bathrobe, a rack of button-down shirts, an ancient red cashmere vest with moth holes. We were just about the same size.

I wasn't ready to face Richard yet. I slipped behind him and went on to the ladies' room. The door was locked, so I waited in an alcove by a painting of a gondola in Venice, the canal bruised blue and black and green.

When the ladies' room was free, I washed my hands. Beneath the brim of Charlotte's hat, my face was smudged, and I took the hat off and carefully splashed water on my face, but still managed to smear my makeup. I wiped the eye shadow and mascara off. Annie would be mad, but I didn't want Richard to think I'd been crying.

When I stepped out of the rest room, Richard was waiting. He stared at me. Blushing, I reached up to adjust the hat.

"The hat's fine," he said. "But where did you dig up that skirt?" He yawned.

"Do you have jet lag?"

He shook his head. "I can't sleep."

"You can't sleep because you drink espresso right before bed. How do you expect to sleep with all that caffeine racing through your bloodstream?"

He laughed. "Ten bucks you stopped to see Mrs. Rapetti," he said.

I didn't answer.

"What's wrong?" he said. "I only meant you sounded like her."

"When I'm with her, I start to sound like her. When I'm with my mother, I sound like my mother. And when I'm with you, I start to sound like you."

Richard ignored that. He always ignored self-deprecating comments.

We sat down at a table by the window. Richard always had to be able to see out; he hated the thought that he might miss something. He set his elbows on the table and leaned his chin on his hands.

"So," he said.

I'd planned a little speech, but suddenly the waiter was hovering, and I couldn't speak. Without asking me what I wanted or looking at the menu, Richard ordered a carafe of wine, two orders of tabbouleh, a hunk of goat's cheese, and a loaf of Swiss peasant bread.

"You better check out the menu," the waiter said, holding an open one toward Richard.

But Richard ignored it. "I told you what I want," he said.

I looked away to keep from laughing. Here was a perfect example of the problem with our relationship: Richard was being obnoxious and I couldn't help thinking it was funny.

"Try the individual pizzas," the waiter suggested. "What about a chef's salad?" He chewed the eraser on the end of his pencil, probably anticipating a scene.

I stood up. "Let's go," I said to Richard.

Relieved, the waiter smiled. Richard smiled, too. On the way out, I turned to make sure he was following me, in time to see him slip a bill into the pocket of the waiter's apron.

Richard's loft was in a neighborhood of warehouses that used to store spices and coffee. In warm weather, an odor rose from the sidewalk which I could never identify precisely —

some combination of India tea, cinnamon, and ginger. Depending on my mood, the smell was either intoxicating or sickening. Richard said it reminded him of the market in Marrakesh.

As I paused for a breath on the third-floor landing of Richard's building, the banister I was leaning on shifted. The staircase was wooden and rickety and looked as if it might collapse any moment, but Richard pushed blithely past me. By the time I made it to his place two flights up, he'd already poured wine for us. "Out of breath?" he said.

"Don't rub it in."

"Not doing your laps?"

I shook my head.

While Richard fixed lunch, I wandered around the loft, investigating. Things were remarkably the same. I picked up a photograph of the two of us on a pink cliff in the Badlands, from the time we drove cross-country. Richard had mounted his camera on a rock, set the timer, and raced to my side before the shutter snapped.

"Remember that trip?" Richard asked, coming up behind me.

"Of course." I set the picture down.

"And Paris, you remember Paris?"

"Sure." Those were the two trips we'd taken together.

Richard looked satisfied, as if he'd proved something. But all he'd proved was that I hadn't forgotten.

When lunch was ready, he carried the tray into his bedroom. I hesitated in the doorway. "It's the only cool place," he said. "Hurry up. Close the door."

Half the air conditioner was mine, as was half the TV. One unseasonably cold winter, Richard and I had decided to splurge on a twenty-six-inch color stereo set with remote control, and the salesman had offered us a good deal if we'd buy an air conditioner, too.

In Richard's room, the only place to sit was on the bed. I perched myself at the foot, while Richard settled himself against the headboard with all the pillows. "Come here," he said, patting the space next to him.

The minute I'd arranged myself beside him, he leaned over, smoothed my hair back from my face, and kissed me. Then he sat up and said, "Marry me."

"What?" I said faintly.

"You heard me."

"What would my grandfather say?" I asked, trying to make a joke of it.

In a voice remarkably like my grandfather's, Richard said, "Of all the idiotic things, that idiot granddaughter of mine ran off with the first idiot who'd have her."

I laughed.

"Say you will." Richard took my hand.

Of course, I thought; but I pulled my hand away. "I can't leave Annie and Sara," I said. "They're just getting used to me."

"That's why it's high time you got out of there," Richard said. "You've helped them through the roughest part. The longer you stay now, the harder it'll be to leave. You'll want to, but your conscience won't let you. You won't want to make them go through losing someone else."

What Richard said made sense, but I shook my head. "I can't explain it."

"Wait a minute," he said. "I think I get it. It's not the girls you're worrying about. It's you. You're not ready."

"Not ready for what?" I said stiffly.

"Not ready to admit that you're still alive."

In the end, we hardly touched our food. Eventually, I got up from the bed and carried the tray to the kitchen. I was about to add our lunch dishes to the pile that was already in the sink, but I'd been trained too well ever to leave a kitchen in that condition.

While the sink was filling with hot sudsy water, I cleared the counters and wiped them clean. I washed the dishes quickly, stacking them neatly in the dish drainer. I covered what was left of the food with plastic wrap and corked the wine bottle. When I was finished, I folded the dish towel over the edge of the sink, carried a kitchen chair into the bathroom, and called Richard to come at once.

When he was seated, I hung a towel around his shoulders and combed his hair. After snipping an inch off the ends, I went to work on the top. To make sure both sides were even, I kept an eye on his face in the mirror, but I didn't meet his gaze.

After the haircut, I pressed Richard's chin to his chest and lathered his neck with shaving cream. With the razor I found in a cup on the sink, I carefully shaved the stubbly hairs. When his skin was smooth, I blotted it dry.

"Done," I said, turning and shaking the towel over the bathtub.

"You know, I thought I saw that kid from your glee club," Richard said.

"Who?"

"You know. The one with legs like toothpicks. Barrettes with little trinkets dangling, little seashells and charms. And socks bunched around her ankles, and her lips pursed in this really serious expression."

"Lydia," I said.

"That's right," Richard said, and his face in the mirror was angry. "The thing is," he went on. "Annie and Sara aren't your kids. Your kids are waiting for you uptown."

There was a long, horrible pause, during which I finally looked Richard in the eye. "Not anymore," I told him. "I mailed my resignation last week."

The moment I walked out of Richard's apartment that day, I wanted to get back in. Suddenly, all I could think of were his best qualities. When we used to go away on weekends together, he worried about his cat being lonely. In photos of the two of us, some part of our bodies was always touching. For a while after I met him, I would still get lost traveling south of the numbered streets, and he bought me a wallet-sized map of the city. On it, he'd made an X at the corner where he lived.

I called my mother from Grand Central and when I got off the train at our station, she was dutifully waiting. "Sara refused to take her top off at the pool," she reported. "Do you think she's self-conscious about gaining weight?"

"I'm putting her on a diet," I said.

"Oh, Lou, a diet? She's only ten. She's just a little chubby, don't you think?"

"Kids are going to start making fun of her." Suddenly, I touched the top of my head, then swung around to look in the back seat.

"What?" said my mother.

"Charlotte's hat. I know I had it on the train."

"It doesn't matter."

"Maybe I dropped it on the platform."

"Oh, Lou, it's late —"

"Please."

She sighed but made a right at the intersection, swinging back through town, past the diner and City Hall. When we reached the station, I retraced my steps. The air was still; the hat couldn't have blown away. It wasn't on the platform or in the waiting room. I even looked in the trash can.

"It must have fallen off on the train," my mother said. "Who'd bother stealing that old thing?"

"I can't remember if I was wearing it or if I put it on the seat. I'll call Lost and Found tomorrow."

When my mother dropped me off at home, Annie was sitting on the front steps. "Well?" she said to me.

I shrugged.

"You shouldn't have changed your clothes. You should have stood up to Grandma. That outfit you had on was a power outfit."

Sara came pounding down the driveway on her pogo stick.

She turned onto the sidewalk, then up the front walk, her pigtail slapping her back. The rubber cap on the end of the pogo stick had worn away, and every time she landed on the exposed metal tip, I flinched.

"What — did — you — bring — me?" she said, timing each word with her impact.

I looked from her to Annie. They were sweet girls, for the most part. "Well?" said Sara, her sweaty face squinting up at me. "What did you buy me?"

"Nothing," I said.

eLeveN

FRED LACEY, SENIOR, never made it to the hospital when his son was being born. He tried to compensate for his negligence by visiting Nora several times a day while she convalesced. "She didn't need him then," my mother said. "She had me to talk to." Instead of reporting to work at the corrugated box factory, where he operated a forklift, he brought Nora Italian chocolates and enormous bouquets — "ostentatious things," according to my mother. "Things he could no more afford than the moon." Three months later, he was gone.

Nora never lost weight after Fred was born. If anything, she seemed to grow larger with every year. She wore her maternity clothes until they wore out, then loose dresses in bright colors. When we were growing up, I'd see her drive by in an orange Volkswagen the same color as her hair. She'd taken a job at the local real estate office.

It was Nora who found Fred the rental for his sabbatical year, a house that no one had been able to sell because the owner couldn't bring herself to chop down the weeping willow tree out front that prevented any light from entering. The house was perfect for Fred, whose eyes teared in the slightest bit of sun. He assigned each small, dark room a purpose. He read in the library, brought company into the parlor. The room hung with Audubon prints was for thinking, he explained, the day he gave the girls and me a tour. He'd invited all three of us to tea, so Sara would get over being jealous about Annie's math lessons.

"What do you think about?" Sara asked him.

He laughed and tugged her braid. "Sometimes I think about you."

"Really?" She turned to me. "Is he just saying that?"

The year he spent in England, Fred had learned to enjoy a cup of tea in the afternoon. For us, he set out cookies and all kinds of sandwiches — Swiss cheese and jelly, chopped chicken liver, cream cheese and pimiento-filled olives. Tea was served in the parlor around a cordovan-topped table. We sat in unmatching, overstuffed armchairs, and the tea service had silver tongs for the sugar, instead of a spoon.

Although he was a large man, Fred looked perfectly at ease sipping tea from a flowery cup. He'd always had a mysterious confidence in himself; at least to me, it was mysterious, because I'd seen him be teased mercilessly as a boy. His mother had dressed him in sport shirts and double-knit trousers when all the other boys were in T-shirts and jeans. She gave him a comb to keep in his back pocket, for tidying his hair after recess. Once, my mother tried to say something to Nora about Fred's clothes, but Nora laughed. "Boys are different than girls, Liz. They don't care what they wear."

She dressed Fred the way her husband used to dress, I supposed, and Fred never seemed to mind. But once he went away to school, he stopped dressing that way. Instead, he wore khaki trousers, soft cotton shirts in pastel colors, and mail-order walking shoes with soles so thick and knobby that he left impressions on the carpet when he crossed a room. It became his uniform; and it still suited him now.

"There are a million kinds of tea," Annie informed Sara and me when Fred had gone to the kitchen. "So far, Fred and I have had Earl Grey, Irish Breakfast, Assam, and Darjeeling. This is Earl Grey, Fred's favorite. It was named for a real earl."

"What's an earl?" asked Sara.

"A rich guy," Annie explained, as Fred returned with a pot of hot water to warm the tea.

"Not necessarily," he said. "A lot of noble families lost their money over the years, and all they had left were their titles.

England is full of lords and counts and earls who are flat broke."

"We don't have titles or nobility or any of that here," I said. "Here, everyone's born equal."

"How come when Fred tells something, it sounds interesting, and when you tell something, it sounds like homework?" Annie asked me.

"Annie!" Fred said. "Don't ever let me hear you use that tone of voice with your aunt again."

Annie blushed and ran out of the room. "I better go talk to her," said Fred.

Sara wanted to go after them, but I wouldn't let her. "Great," she said. "Why do I always get stuck with you?" She bounced on the cushion of the chair.

Later, when we were leaving, I sent the girls on ahead and thanked Fred for defending me. "I didn't mean to jump in where I don't belong," he said. "But she made me mad. What she said isn't the slightest bit true."

To show Annie that all was forgiven, Fred had presented her with a bar of soap that smelled like raspberries. On the way home, she said, "Why can't we have soaps like this, instead of plain Ivory?"

Fred had begun to give us things. Everywhere he went, it seemed, something caught his eye that I or one of the girls or my mother had to have. After I'd mentioned that one thing I missed about the city was being able to buy exotic fruit any time of year, Fred brought me a kiwi and a mango. He gave Annie pink socks with poodles on them. He bought an inflatable air mattress for my mother to take along on her trip down the Amazon. One day, he arrived with a gift for Sam — a bottle of port.

For Sara, Fred found a policeman's regulation flashlight, and from then on, Sara shone the thing everywhere. At night, long after she should have been asleep, I'd hear her padding around. Once she wakened before dawn so she could pick out her clothes by her flashlight's beam, and when she crept downstairs, she scared Sam half to death.

Sara began spending her free time in the attic, using the flashlight to poke through her parents' old things. One afternoon she found a diary stuffed in a box with some faded beach towels and tank suits. She came downstairs to ask me if it was okay to read it.

"I forgot your mother kept a diary," I said. "That must be where you get it from."

The leather cover was antique white with gold embossed trim. Sara sat down beside me on the couch and jimmied the lock with a pin. "January second," she read. "Dear Diary, I meant to start writing in you yesterday, but I forgot till I was already in bed, and if I write with my flashlight under the covers the lines come out crooked."

Sara closed the diary and looked at me. "I forgot about her flashlight," I said. "She used to wait until I fell asleep, then shine it in my face."

"Did you two fight?" asked Sara.

"Sure."

"Like me and Annie?"

"Annie and me," I corrected her. "Worse."

"Much worse?"

"Your mother was a pincher," I said.

"But pinching's dirty fighting."

"I pulled her hair."

"That's dirty, too," said Sara. "Who won?"

"She did. She was always bigger," I said, and that seemed to satisfy Sara.

The morning after Annie's math exam, Sam and the girls flew to California to visit his parents. Fred and I drove them to the airport, and on the way, Annie described in detail problems from her exam.

"The third one was a collision," she said from the back seat, where she was squeezed between Sara and Sam. "One train going east at sixty miles per hour, another going west at eighty-five. They're on the same track. When will they crack up, if they're one hundred miles apart now?"

"What are they doing on the same track?" I said. "Why aren't the conductors watching where they're going? Why can't they stop in time?"

"Which formula did you use?" Fred asked, glancing over his shoulder to see if he could change lanes.

"Distance equals rate times time," Annie said.

He nodded. "Then there was an airplane version," she said. "I used the same formula."

"Good girl," said Fred.

"Do they crash?" Sara said. "I bet they crash."

"Could we please change the subject?" I said.

"Don't be so superstitious, Aunt Lou."

"I gave the office my folks' number," Sam said, tapping my shoulder. "But if anyone calls me, tell them I'll call back the next day."

"Daddy, are you going to be working the whole time?" Annie asked.

"Not the whole time."

"You better not leave us alone with Grandma," Annie said. "I never know what to say."

"Just listen," I advised her. "Nod. Say, 'Really?'"

"We all know what you do," Annie said.

I turned around. "Is there something wrong with that?"

"You're supposed to know what to say."

"Don't criticize your aunt," Sam said.

"It's okay," I told him.

But he shook his head. "It's not okay with me."

At the airport, Fred and I waved from behind the velvet rope until Sam and the girls boarded the plane. As we walked back through the terminal, I said, "So, do you think Annie's going to pass?"

"I wish we'd had more time," Fred said. "She needed more drill with word problems."

"You're wonderful to have helped her. You did a great job. You gave her confidence."

"We were working against the clock."

Once outside the terminal, we dragged along in the humidity and exhaust. "The AC will kick on in just a minute," Fred promised, when we reached his car. He took his cap off and set it on the dashboard, then rubbed his eyes. I suspected that he was working on his book late into the night, to make up for the time he was spending with Annie and Sara. He was over at our house practically every single day, it seemed, and I didn't know how to stop it, or whether I even wanted to. He made my life easier.

Halfway home, a car ahead of us pulled off the highway, steam spiraling from its hood. "Poor guy," said Fred.

"That's a nice thing about Sam," I said. "He always stops to help cars in distress. It used to drive Charlotte crazy. Sometimes it took them twice as long to get places."

Fred turned to me, frowning. "There was nothing I could do. He was overheated, that's all. Nothing to do but sit it out."

"I didn't mean *you* should have stopped," I said.

Approaching the tollbooth, Fred slowed and reached in the coin holder on the dashboard. "I'd like to get to know Sam."

"I wish I could help you," I said. "I used to think I knew him. We used to have lunch once in a while. The school where I taught wasn't far from his office. And sometimes, he came over to my apartment after work with potato chips and Coke — things Charlotte wouldn't allow in the house."

"He seems like a nice guy," Fred said.

"I have a funny feeling he may be spending time with Nan Gordon," I said.

Fred nodded. "I bumped into them one night walking home from the station. They'd had dinner in the city."

"Oh," was all I said.

Fred glanced over. "It's probably nothing," he said. "Nan Gordon doesn't hold a candle to Charlotte."

We were quiet the next few miles. Then, as he was pulling up the exit ramp, Fred said, "Boy did I have a crush on her."

.   .   .

The spring Charlotte and Fred were in eighth grade, he asked her out practically every single weekend, in person. The first time, he'd saved up weeks of his allowance for store-bought flowers. "They smell like soap," Charlotte had said, wrinkling her nose. Fred was on the front step, and I was behind the door, giggling into my palm.

"What sort of flowers do you like?" Fred had asked, taking a pad and pencil from his seat pocket. Back then, he never went anyplace without a pad and pencil.

"Black-eyed Susans," Charlotte had told him, taken by surprise. "Tiger lilies." She hadn't meant to encourage him. She was always careful with Fred because he was Nora's son. The next weekend, he showed up with a ragged bouquet and red, dripping eyes from picking flowers in the woods behind his house. Charlotte had to say no, over and over.

When he was seven, Fred had begun reading the *World Book* encyclopedia, and he finished the XYZ volume in fourth grade. In car pool, he asked questions only he knew how to answer, questions like: What started the Franco-Prussian War? Know where Oman is? When did the trilobites go extinct?

When other boys were trading baseball cards and playing kick ball and teasing girls, Fred had moved on to the Bible. He courted Charlotte with his knowledge. How old was Joshua when he died? What did the Queen of Sheba bestow on Solomon? What were the colors of the tapestry that hung at the gate of the tabernacle?

"Blue, purple, and scarlet," he told Charlotte, but she just stared. He couldn't capture her imagination, but I was fascinated by someone so smart, although I'd never have admitted it to Charlotte.

"Now, you know Pop and Aunt Clara would love to have us for a visit," my mother said over the telephone the next morning. I was talking on the extension phone, still in bed. Ordinarily, I would have been up by this time, but I hadn't slept well in the empty house, silent except when the sump pump exhaled. Only an hour after Fred dropped me off, I'd begun to miss the girls. A stack of books on my night table, a pattern for gabardine trousers by the sewing machine — that was what lay ahead of me the next two weeks.

"It's too buggy at the lake in August," I said.

"You're right. Anyway, I don't want to hear any more about this trip. What have I gotten myself into, going down the Amazon with Aunt Clara? All I wanted to do was shock Pop. That's the only reason I said I'd go."

"It'll be an experience," I told her.

"Just what I need. Do you want to go to the pool this afternoon? Adult swim begins at three. I need the exercise. Should I pick you up or do you want to come get me? No, I'll get you — I need to stop for some gas."

We reached the pool a little early, and the teenagers were still there, lolling on inner tubes and rafts, the girls in bikinis and sunglasses, the boys in cutoff jeans. "We could do some sewing for Annie and Sara, I suppose," my mother said, stretching out. "It'll be September before you know it."

The lifeguard slid his sunglasses to the tip of his nose and yelled at a boy who was running. The kid halted, then tiptoed to the edge of the pool and cannonballed into the water. The guard blew his whistle. "No cannonballs, no splashing, no horseplay!"

The boy swam underwater toward a girl whose hair was carefully tucked back in a bandanna. He disappeared beneath her pink, puffy raft, then surfaced, upending it. She came up, sputtering, "Edward Jason McCauley, your ass is grass!" As she swam in quick little breast strokes toward him, her bandanna slid off and rippled on the surface of the water like a flag.

The lifeguard blew his whistle furiously, but it was war — boys against girls. Rafts and tubes flew in the air, water churned.

"Kids," said my mother.

"Next year, Annie will be one of those girls," I predicted.

"Remember Charlotte?" said my mother. "She spent all morning getting ready to come to the pool — eye shadow, the works, her shorts just so. She came home looking like a drowned raccoon. You were the one with sense."

I remembered that summer, my last before high school. If I could have lured Charlotte away from the pool, it would have been perfect. I didn't ache to grow up, the way she did. But the few times she stayed home, she'd be bored and snappish by noon, and I'd wish she wasn't there. Without her, my mother and I could drift along in our hazy routine of yard sales and long hours in the sewing room. I tried on my fall clothes and Charlotte's. My mother knew exactly how a dress should look on me to fit Charlotte, the skirt to the middle of my calves, the sleeves below my fingertips. While my mother ran the sewing machine, I kept our glasses full of lemonade.

That summer Charlotte had stopped letting my mother fix her hair. She rolled it herself with frozen orange juice cans so it hung as limp as a spaniel's ears. The last night of vacation I shook my head when my mother offered to do my hair specially. I waited until she was busy cutting coupons from the evening paper, then slowly climbed the stairs.

After Charlotte finished her hair, she rolled mine. She'd been saving up extra cans for me. In bed, she said, "You'll get used to it. You'll fall asleep. You'll be glad. This is how everyone's going to be wearing their hair this year."

"What should we have for supper?" my mother asked me as we were leaving the pool.

I bent to dislodge a pebble from my thong.

"Don't be so enthusiastic," she said. "Maybe we should barbecue. Do I have any charcoal left? I can't remember if I bought a new bag the last time I went to the supermarket."

"We have some," I said. "And there's a London broil in the freezer we could defrost."

"No red meat for me," my mother said.

"You're serious about this diet."

"I had dinner with Nora last night and I watched the way she eats. I don't want the same thing happening to me." She started the engine. We heard a futile chug, then silence. She turned the key in the ignition again, and the car rumbled feebly. "It won't do that when I bring it to Sunoco," she said. "I told Ned there's something wrong with the starter, or about to be wrong, but he said no, and charged me fifty bucks. Ned only listens to your father."

In our family, there'd always been male tasks and female tasks. After dropping us at the entrance to the pool, my father would go park the car in the lot while my mother and Charlotte and I changed into bathing suits in the mildewed locker room. At Christmas, he strung lights and left the balls and tinsel for us. Pulling on a jacket to carry the garbage out on cold nights, he'd leave us laughing in the steamy kitchen. Years ago, he'd begun to slip away. From the time we were small, Charlotte and I had gotten used to leaving him alone. "Daddy had a rough day," my mother would say, and he'd sit all by himself in the living room, reading the newspaper.

My mother pressed the accelerator and listened. "Now it sounds okay. Let's drive out to Rafferty's and buy some fish for dinner."

"All the way out there?"

"What else do we have to do?"

"There must be something."

"Face it," my mother said, braking at the parking lot exit. "We have nothing to do."

"The girls will be back," I said.

She shook her head. "I'm going to get a job. That's what I was talking to Nora about last night. She wants me to come work at Sheffield and Son. She says I'd pick up sales in no time. I could work with her, learn the ropes, then take my real estate exam next spring. All those developments and condos out behind the mall, and Nora says they're going to be building high rises along the river in the next few years. It's a growing market. People always need places to live."

"Would you really like doing that?" I asked.

"It's better than doing nothing."

That evening we grilled swordfish, and afterward sat on my mother's porch, watching neighbors and their dogs walk by. "I don't know a soul on this street anymore," my mother said. "Everyone else moved once their kids grew up."

"You should get out more," she said a little while later. "Meet people." She gestured toward the houses across the street, but all the doors and windows were closed. Everyone around but my mother had central air conditioning. She complained that my father was too cheap.

"You're not giving off the right signals," my mother went on. "You should dress up a little. You can look so nice when you try." She glanced at me. "What about Richard? Have you heard from him since you had lunch?"

I shrugged.

"I can't read your mind, you know," she said.

When I didn't answer, she snorted in exasperation and went inside. Soon she came out again, smelling of perfume. "Come on, let's walk to town. We'll have an ice cream. Ice cream will cheer us up, and I won't feel so guilty if we walk."

As we started out, she said, "Aunt Clara sent me a list. Shots. Mosquito netting. Where on earth do I buy mosquito netting?"

"Fred will know."

"Stop me the next time I open my big mouth in front of Pop," said my mother.

"Maybe Aunt Clara will change her mind."

"Unfortunately, Aunt Clara has never once not done what she said she was going to do."

"You could tell her you changed your mind."

My mother shook her head. "If I back out now, Pop won't let me forget it the rest of my life."

At the ice cream parlor, Fred was sitting at a table in the back corner. He waved for us to come over. Before joining him, my mother ordered a sundae, although she said she shouldn't, and I asked for a dish of lemon sherbet. After giving Fred his usual kiss, my mother said, "Nora sold a house today."

"The couple from Memphis?" Fred whistled. "That was a hard sell. They kept comparing prices here to down in Tennessee."

"Your mother could sell a fur coat to a bear," my mother replied.

The waitress arrived with our order. "This one," said my mother, nodding toward me, "drives me crazy. Lemon sherbet. She's the epitome of restraint."

"I wish I was," Fred said, taking a bite of his sundae. "By the way, Mom's birthday is on Friday. I thought the four of us could go to Jack's for dinner."

"I won't pretend I have to consult my engagement calendar," my mother said. She held out a spoonful of ice cream. "You've got to at least help me with this, Lou."

I took a bite, then asked Fred how his book was coming along.

"Actually, I've been sitting here trying to figure something out," he said. "Kant says that man is free because his will is governed by reason, and that rational beings are lawgivers to themselves. But man isn't only rational, he's natural. What happens when those two impulses come into conflict? And what if an individual's laws are different from the laws of society?"

"There can only be one set of laws," my mother said. "Otherwise there would be chaos. Someone famous must have said that. People have to be responsible."

"Responsibility — that brings up another interesting question. Freud says —"

"I don't care what Freud says," my mother interrupted. "You're starting to sound like Phillip, always quoting his psychiatrist. I'll tell you what I tell him every single time we talk. You do not desert your family. Period."

Fred looked grave. "Oh, honey," my mother began, probably remembering that she wasn't the only person sitting at the table to have been deserted, but Fred had gone back to eating, his spoon clicking back and forth between the glass bowl and his teeth.

Since Fred and I were kids, Jack has been running his steak house on the Hudson. Before that, his father had been the boss, importing waitresses from the city with bright lipstick and marcelled hair. According to my mother, it used to be a dark, musty roadhouse until Jack took over and renovated the place with full-length sliding doors on the riverside.

On Friday night, Jack greeted Fred, Nora, my mother, and me at the door. "Happy birthday, doll," he said, kissing Nora's cheek.

"Ooh, we clash," she cried. "Don't get too close." Her dress was emerald green silk, and Jack, a slender man with an over-sized mustache, was wearing a lavender shirt.

"We're a little hectic in the kitchen tonight," Jack said. "Our salad girl walked out. I've been recruited to chop tomatoes." He patted Fred's shoulder. "Any problems, just holler. Have the porterhouse. I'll see you folks later."

When our drinks arrived, I lifted my glass. "Good news," I said. "Mrs. Green called."

"Annie passed?" said my mother.

"What'd she get?" Fred asked.

"A seventy-seven."

He set his drink down. "That's not even a B."

"It's better than an F," my mother said. "We're not a family of perfectionists."

Nora laughed. "I'm no perfectionist, either. I don't know where Freddy gets it from."

"That's why he's so successful," my mother said. "He has to get everything just right."

"Make sure you don't let Annie know how you feel," I said to Fred. "She'd be heartbroken. She's buying you a present to say thank you."

"She wasn't disappointed?"

"She sounded like an enormous weight had been lifted from her shoulders."

"Well, that makes me feel a little better."

"Looks like someone's going to find a job tomorrow," said Nora, picking the slimy root of a radish from her salad.

"Maybe I should take it," said my mother. "Making a salad is one thing I know how to do."

"I want you at Sheffield and Son," Nora said. "You'd be fabulous. You're very persuasive."

"Not to Phillip, I'm not," my mother said. "I give him reasons A to Z why he should come home, and nothing works."

"Men aren't logical," Nora said. "House buyers are. You can share my listings."

"I almost forgot." My mother raised her wine glass. "Here's to Nora, for selling the Mastersons' house."

"It was pure luck," Nora said. "There we were in the backyard with the sun pouring down, and suddenly, a little bird started chirping and melted their hearts. I could have kissed that bird."

"If I took a job, I'd have an excuse for not going down the Amazon with Aunt Clara," my mother said.

"I wouldn't entertain an idea like going down the Amazon for one minute," Nora said.

"Believe me, it was a foolish gesture. My father brings out the idiot in me."

Our table overlooked the river, and as we ate I watched the sun setting on the water. Up here, the Hudson curved, graceful as a ribbon. I'd seen its source — Lake Tear of the Clouds in the Adirondacks. One summer, my family had taken a camping trip there. "Everything has a beginning and an end," I remembered my father saying.

As we were studying the dessert menu, Jack hurried over in a splattered apron. "Well, folks, how was everything?" he asked.

"Out of this world," said Nora.

"I'd love to stay and chat, but I'm up to my elbows in lettuce. Know anyone looking for a job?"

My mother leaned forward, her face flushed. "I am," she announced. "And I've got credentials, too. Fifty years, I've been making salads."

Jack laughed politely.

"I'm serious," she insisted. "Lou here can tell you I make a nice salad. You think I'm drunk? Well, maybe I am, but I'm serious too. Aren't I, Nora?"

"I'm serious about wanting you at Sheffield and Son," Nora said.

My mother shook her head. "I want to work where I'm comfortable — in a kitchen, chopping."

After dinner, instead of leaving as we'd arrived — my mother and I in her car, Nora and Fred in his — Fred took me home, and Nora drove my mother's car. "I could have driven Mom," I said to Fred, watching the two women pull out of the parking lot ahead of us.

"My mother can try to persuade her not to take that job."

"I've never seen her get like that before," I said, a little while later.

"We're all a bit drunk," Fred said.

"She was practically flirting with Jack."

"You could take a few lessons from your mother. You're grim as a bear."

Fred turned right at Montgomery Street and drove up the block. "Sorry," he said, stopping in front of my house. "I'm drunk, too. And I'm happy about Annie," he went on. "I admit I was a tiny bit disappointed at first, but that's all gone now."

"Sam and I are grateful to you." I reached for the handle of the door.

"Wait." Fred's face drifted toward me, his eyes fervent as a preacher's. "You're not drunk, are you? You're not the slightest bit drunk."

I opened the door.

"What are you hanging on to?" he whispered.

twelve

THE FIRST MORNING the girls were home from California they spent making a list of things they needed for school — notebooks, pens, erasers, loose-leaf binders, Magic Markers, book straps, sneakers for gym, smocks for art class, new ballet slippers.

"I need an assignment pad, too," said Annie, on our way to the stationery store. "Where's the list? I'm going to buy only pink things this year, even pink pens."

In the store I admired an extra-large collection of crayons with a built-in sharpener. "Coloring's for babies," Sara said, putting her hands behind her back.

"But look how beautiful," I said. "Just the names are beautiful. Periwinkle, russet, magenta." I laid the box in the shopping basket.

"No," Sara said, quickly taking it out. "Everyone'll think they're for me."

"Better get yourself a baby, Aunt Lou," said Annie. "Then you can buy crayons."

Sara flushed, and disappeared around the corner to the next aisle. Annie giggled. "Grandma asked me if you'd given Sara that talk."

"I guess it's time," I said.

Sara had celebrated her eleventh birthday in California. Sam's parents gave her a leopard-print bathing suit, which she immediately turned over to Annie, and a trip to Disneyland. There were photographs of Sara shaking hands with Minnie Mouse and Pluto.

"Do you think she knows?" I asked Annie.

Annie shrugged. "I tried telling her once, but she wouldn't listen." Annie picked up a tube of silver glitter. "Some girls glue this stuff to their chests," she said.

"What?"

"You know. Right here." She tapped her collarbone. "When they go out. So it looks like stardust. It's sexy." She dropped the glitter into the basket and marched ahead of me down the aisle.

The next day Sara was snooping in the attic again and came downstairs lugging a large suitcase. "What do you have there?" I asked. I was sitting on the couch with a book about sex, which I'd bought to teach Sara, and I quickly put it aside.

Sara laid the suitcase on the floor and opened it. Inside were old dolls, Charlotte's and mine. It was odd that Charlotte had ended up with them. When we were kids, I was the one who couldn't bear to give any of my dolls away; Charlotte would discard an old one every time she received a brand-new one. Because of that, my doll family was extensive, made up of mine and Charlotte's castoffs.

Before giving a doll away, Charlotte would always cut its hair or perform surgery. "I'm afraid Annabel needs an immediate appendectomy," she'd say. I'd run and get my mother's manicure scissors while Charlotte scrubbed up. When she said, "Scissors," I'd slap them against her palm the way the nurses did on *Dr. Kildare* and watch her struggle to make a cut in the hard plastic belly.

"I'm too old for these," Sara said, wistfully adjusting a dress on one of the dolls.

"Come here a minute," I said, reaching for the book.

It turned out that Sara already knew about sex, but she had questions. "So they do it when they want to have a baby?" she said.

"Well, no," I said. "They do it often because they love each other."

Sara stared down at one of the illustrations in the book and traced her finger around the woman's head and shoulders and breasts. "Why are her eyes shut?" she asked. "Is she sleeping?"

I shook my head. "She's enjoying herself."

Sara fidgeted. We were sitting side by side on the couch, the book open across our laps. "But then she can't see."

"You don't have to see," I said. "You feel."

"Feel what?"

"Warm," I said. "And your heart beats faster, and then you feel a kind of rushing throughout your entire body, and then you feel a kind of explosion —"

"Like dynamite?" she said eagerly.

"No, no, it's all inside, it's like —" I closed the book.

"Like when someone has a heart attack?" Sara asked.

"I don't know. I've never had a heart attack."

"But you've had sex, right?"

I nodded.

"I'm going upstairs now," Sara said.

"Here, take this." I held out the book, and she tucked it under her arm. I knew she was going straight to her room to write everything I'd said in her diary, which meant that Sam would eventually find out what I'd told her. That was the only way he and I seemed to communicate these days.

On the first day of school, I woke as the sun was rising, pink spilling onto the sidewalks. A moment later, it was over, everything back to normal, the colors adjusting themselves the way they do on a TV screen.

Sam was up early, too. That afternoon, he was leaving for Japan on business. The girls had traced their feet on cardboard, and Sam had measured their heights, so he could buy them zori and kimonos for their Halloween costumes.

"Morning," I said. Sam nodded but didn't reply. He was counting tablespoons of coffee into the filter. "We could get one of those coffee machines that go on automatically," I said. "They do everything, even grind the beans. Coffee's ready when you come downstairs."

"But I like making coffee," Sam said. He poured boiling water through the filter and sat down to wait.

"Are you packed? Can I help with anything? Do you have enough shirts?"

"I'm all set," he said.

"Are you sure I can't iron something?"

He shook his head. "One thing," he said, reaching in the pocket of his bathrobe. "I wrote out a list of numbers where you can reach me. And you can always call my secretary. She'll know how to get a hold of me."

"I'm sure we won't need to," I said.

Sam sighed. "I guess not."

When the coffee was ready, I carried my cup outside and sat down on the porch steps. Fred happened to be running by just then, in red jogging shorts and a cap. Seeing me, he trotted over, his chin and forehead glistening. The visor of his cap, a present from Annie, read "Disneyland — Love It or Leave It."

I went inside to get him a glass of water. When I handed it to him, he gulped the water down, his shoulders curving forward. He was so broad and powerful that he could have been an athlete. Everything about Fred was excessive. His voice reverberated, even when he was out of breath, and it was a wonder he could find sneakers large enough for his feet.

"Next year, I'm going to run the marathon," he announced.

"That's over twenty miles," I said.

He unfastened the pedometer around his waist. "Only nine point six."

"Nine point six miles? You must have been up before dawn."

He nodded. "I woke up thinking, Today's the first day of school, and for the first time since I was four, I'm not going."

I couldn't tell from his tone of voice how he felt about that. "Do you wish you were back in Boston?" I asked.

He smiled. "Not at all," he said.

.   .   .

It was sheet-changing day. I stripped the beds and carried the bundle down to the basement. The plain white sheets were Annie's; designs and colors gave her nightmares, she said. Sara's sheets had Raggedy Anns tumbling all over. Mine were mauve with purple daisies. "Hideous," Charlotte had said, when she spotted them in the bargain basement of a department store, shopping one day with me. "But I guess they'll do for guests," she decided.

While the sheets were in the wash, I telephoned my mother. "Can't talk now," she said. "Jack just called. He's adding a chef's salad to the menu. I have to practice my julienning."

"Jack this, Jack that," I said.

After we hung up, I went out back with another cup of coffee and wandered over to the garden. Weeds had strangled the Sweet William, and the hollyhocks had withered without blossoming. Even the zinnias looked stunted.

I tugged at a slender, translucent stem with tiny yellow flowers which I thought was a weed. If I'd paid attention to Charlotte, I'd have known for certain. But I never listened. All she ever wanted to talk about, it seemed, was the garden. She'd stopped reading novels in favor of books by horticulture experts. In time, she became a bit of an expert herself. For a few years, she even wrote a gardening column in the local newspaper. She stopped, though, when she received a letter that began, "Because of your so-called advice, my entire tomato crop was ruined." For a while after that, she was reluctant to make suggestions about anything.

"It's a little late," said Nan Gordon, sidling through the hedge.

"I thought I'd tidy up a bit."

"I wasn't going to say anything," she said. "I was going to hold my tongue. But I can't. Charlotte had the most beautiful garden in town. You haven't been back here once. I've watched you walk out the door, straight to the garage, without a glance in this direction. Charlotte would be furious with you."

I grabbed what I hoped was a weed, my hand trembling. Nan was probably right. Charlotte had never walked through the yard without stopping to yank weeds. Spring through fall, her fingernails were caked with dirt.

"Those flowers meant more to Charlotte than anything," Nan practically shrieked.

She was describing the same Charlotte who used to worry about the working conditions of the waiters in Chinese restaurants while everyone else was enjoying the egg foo yung. I could remember Charlotte saying, "I have to do what I have to do, and you have to do what you have to do." I'd thought that meant it mattered what we did.

But somewhere along the way, our lives had shrunk. Charlotte became as fanatic about building up her compost heap as she'd ever been about fighting injustice. She worried about the pH of her soil, and put out cups of beer to drown the slugs. Now I took care of her children because she hadn't been careful enough to stay alive. And I was no better. My life had meant so little to me that the first chance I got, I walked out on it.

By the time I was through pulling everything up from the ground, Nan was nowhere in sight. In minutes, I'd destroyed Charlotte's garden. When I finished, my hands were raw and I felt no triumph. How could I ever have thought that tired patch of earth was my enemy?

"I almost won class secretary," Sara told me first thing when she came through the door at lunchtime that day. "But Mary Ellen Geller got one more vote than me."

"You would have been good," I said. "You have lovely penmanship."

"Mary Ellen makes big G's like this." Sara sketched on the kitchen table. "You're supposed to make them like this," she said, demonstrating. "The teacher told me I had to be a good sport."

"Does your teacher seem nice? What's her name?"

"Mrs. Fletcher. She's nice, but the way she said I should be a good sport was like I was being a bad one. And when I went up to her desk after the bell rang to say I wasn't, she said we had nothing more to discuss."

"I can't stand teachers like that."

Sara shrugged. "Sometimes I get on people's nerves," she said.

As I laughed, I wondered what I was going to do next year when Sara started eating lunch at school instead of coming home for an hour in the middle of the day.

The phone rang. It was Fred. "I wanted to make sure you weren't feeling lonely your first day home alone again."

"I'm not alone. Sara's here."

"Who is it?" Sara wanted to know.

"Fred."

"I have to ask him something."

I passed Sara the phone. While she chatted, I opened to the classified section of the newspaper. There were productive things I could be doing.

After Sara went back to school that afternoon, I sat down at Charlotte's old upright. Some of the keys were chipped, the ivory yellowed and worn. A few of the notes in the upper scales stuck, so your fingers sank in silence. I hadn't touched the piano since the girls' ballet recital last spring. I'd made mistakes that night, though only Nan seemed to notice. Now I positioned my hands above the keys; but something inside me kept them from landing.

thirteen

THE AFTERNOON in late September when my grandfather telephoned, I was sitting around doing nothing. He'd been trying to reach my mother, but she had already left for work. While he was telling me as best he could what had happened, I reached for a pencil and wrote the girls a note saying I'd be home soon.

At Jack's restaurant, I swung open the kitchen door and found him saying to my mother, "Your arms, when you're slicing, send chills down my spine —"

Seeing me, my mother laid her knife down on the counter and wiped her hands on her aproned hips. "Is it Phillip?" she said quietly.

I shook my head. "Aunt Clara. A stroke. Grandpa's going to call back when he knows more. He wants to bring her to the city to see a specialist."

"Pop never trusted the doctors up there," my mother said. "He thought Mom might have had a chance if only they could have moved her." She opened a drawer and passed me a knife. "Do you mind giving me a hand?"

Because she was calm, I was calm. She and Jack and I formed an assembly line at the butcher block counter, and in no time, we had put together fifty salads. I could see why my mother liked working in the kitchen; it was clean and quiet and it smelled good.

"That's enough, don't you think?" my mother said to Jack.

"Sure. You go ahead, Liz."

But she began laying long strips of damp paper toweling

across the rows of salad bowls until Jack took the roll away from her. "I'm kicking you out of here," he said.

As we stood in the parking lot before getting into our cars, I noticed that my mother had worn puffy aerobic sneakers to work, which made her feet look enormous. She clicked the clasp of her purse open and shut. "People recover from strokes every day," she finally said.

The moment the girls saw our cars pulling into the driveway, they jumped up from the steps and raced over. "It's Aunt Clara, but she's going to be fine," my mother called out the window.

"Was it a car accident?" asked Annie.

"No. Something to do with her heart. We'll find out exactly when Pop calls back."

"I'm going to pray," Sara announced. "I think we should all pray."

"Are you turning into a Jesus freak?" Annie asked.

"I'm going to start going to church again," Sara said.

"No one's stopping you," said Annie.

"Don't you think we all should?" Sara turned and asked me.

I hadn't been to church, except on Christmas, since I was sixteen, the year my parents told Charlotte and me it was up to us from then on. Charlotte had stopped going, too, but as soon as Annie was born, she started again, and both babies were baptized in the same christening gown that Charlotte and I had worn. When I accused Charlotte of being a hypocrite, she said, "When you have kids, you'll understand."

"Sara, if you want to go to church, I'll take you," my mother offered.

But Sara said, "Annie has to go, too."

"You should talk to Fred," said Annie. "His book's about how everyone has free will. I get to make my own decisions."

"But Mom wanted us to go," Sara insisted.

"That was before," said Annie.

"But Annie," Sara said. "What if you're wrong? What if we're the only ones who don't get to heaven?"

"I don't want to go to heaven."

"But what if Mom's waiting for us up there?"

"Excuse me," said my mother, making her way past them. "I think I hear the phone."

She didn't run for it. Her steps weren't bouncy as she climbed the porch steps. She looked like an old lady in sneakers, not someone whose arms could send shivers down a man's spine.

As soon as Aunt Clara could be moved, my grandfather brought her down to a hospital in the city. He planned to stay at my mother's house until he could bring Aunt Clara home again. The afternoon he arrived, I stopped over to visit. My grandfather was sitting by the fireplace in a straight-back chair, the most uncomfortable seat in the house.

"Grandpa, why don't you sit over there?" I said, pointing to the soft, old couch, but he turned and gave me a long, nasty look.

"Pop's back is bothering him," my mother said quickly.

"I made lemon squares." I held out the plate.

"Those look scrumptious," said my mother. "Don't they, Pop?" He was silent. "I could use a cup of tea," she went on. "That's what we need — a pick-me-up, right, Pop?"

"Exactly how excited am I supposed to get about a cup of tea?" he asked.

In my mother's kitchen, waiting for the water to boil, I stared out the window. The dogwood had reddened like apples. I tried to remember what Charlotte used to do with the fallen leaves in her backyard. Cover the flower beds? Make mulch? Maybe Sam would know.

My mother hurried into the kitchen and reached for the cardigan she kept on a hook by the door. "I'm getting some logs. Pop's going to start a fire. It's chilly."

"How'd it go at the hospital?" I asked.

"The doctor wanted to do some tests before giving us a prognosis," she said. "Aunt Clara's age is against her, of course, but he said he'd never seen a ninety-year-old looking more fit."

"All that swimming," I said.

My mother nodded. "She can't pinch an inch."

My mother hurried out to get logs, and by the time I carried the tea tray into the living room, my grandfather was squatting in front of the fireplace.

"Do you need more kindling?" my mother asked him.

"Nope." He settled back on his haunches and blew, his lips disappearing into a long O.

"So I hear the doctor was optimistic," I said.

"That's bull," my grandfather said. "What he said was he'd have to wait and see the test results before he could give an opinion."

"Dr. Mitchell is the best neurologist in the country," my mother said.

"Says who?" my grandfather wanted to know.

"Says Dr. Finch, when I talked to him yesterday."

"Dr. Finch wouldn't know a gallbladder from a golf ball."

"I'm sure Aunt Clara's in good hands." My mother held out a cup of tea to my grandfather. "Here. It's chamomile."

But he ignored her and stood up and began to pace around the room.

"Pop, you've got to relax," she said. "We don't want anything happening to you. Did you remember your pills? Come on, sit down, have a lemon square."

"She was sitting there, perfectly normal — if you could ever call Clara normal — then, she started in about a bonfire. 'Sweet Jesus,' I said to her. 'Who's supposed to rake the leaves?' She said, 'Father says don't let Milly get close, she doesn't know any better. We have to watch for Milly.'"

"Who's Milly?" my mother asked.

"There is no Milly," my grandfather said. "She's confusing us with someone else's family. She's had so many different families she can't keep them straight. What kind of woman gets married three times? Clara never could get anything right."

"Wait," said my mother. "Wasn't Milly that cousin of yours who drowned at the picnic?"

"That was Molly." My grandfather poked the fire. "These logs are damp. You must have a leaky tarp, Liz."

"What do you mean? That tarp's brand-new. Phil only bought it last winter."

"You ought to check it."

"If there's a leak, I'm bringing it straight back to Sears. There's no excuse."

My grandfather stood up again and walked in a circle around the hooked rug. "What I don't understand," he said, "is how someone can be perfectly fine one moment, and sick enough to be hospitalized the next."

"Well, Pop —" my mother began.

"What?" My grandfather stopped in front of her. "What pearl of wisdom do you have for me now?"

"Think of her age. The amazing thing is that she's been in such good health up till now."

My grandfather shook his head. "*You* may expect things to go wrong. *You* may take everything lying down. But I'm not going to. Not when it's my only sister we're talking about. That doctor is going to make her well again, or he'll have me to answer to."

Just as the girls and I were sitting down to dinner that evening, Fred stopped by. He'd heard about Aunt Clara from Nora and wanted to know if there was anything he could do to help. I told him he was welcome to stay and eat.

He quickly accepted the invitation. "What smells so good?"

"Tarragon," Annie said glumly. She was mad at her boyfriend about something, but she didn't want to talk about it. To take her mind off him, I'd put her in charge of cooking the chicken.

While we were eating, Fred said, "I know I've met your grandfather. Years ago, one Christmas. But I don't really remember him."

"He's tallish," I said. "He's always worn thick black-rimmed glasses."

"He's bald," said Sara. "But you can't tease him."

"Never," I agreed.

"He's always in a bad mood," Sara went on. "He calls Aunt Clara and Grandma idiots."

"He calls everyone idiots," Annie said.

To be fair, I said, "He doesn't really mean it."

"He's a pain in the ass," Annie said, and Sara nodded.

"Enough," I told them. "Fred gets the picture."

Annie had a wicked glint in her eye. "There was an article in the newspaper today about Richard," she said to me. "You didn't tell me there was going to be a sex scene in his movie."

"I didn't know."

"It's going to be rated R because of that."

"I know," I said. "I read that article, too." I passed the platter of chicken to Fred. "Here, take that last piece."

"Yeah, it's a breast," Annie said. She and Sara went into a fit of giggles.

"Who's Richard?" Fred asked, ignoring the chicken.

Before I could answer, Annie stopped laughing long enough to say, "You're not the only one who wants to screw Aunt Lou."

My grandfather didn't like my mother working at the restaurant. "Why do you need a job?" he asked her. "Explain it again. Isn't Phil supporting you anymore?"

"We share his pension and his social security," she said. "I work for my sense of well-being and self-respect."

"You might explain to me how working in someone else's kitchen is going to give you self-respect," my grandfather said.

The nights my mother worked, I invited my grandfather over for dinner. The girls didn't like it, because he didn't approve of eating in the kitchen, which meant they had to go to the trouble of setting the dining room table, and no one could move until my grandfather finished eating or he'd be annoyed. He was notoriously slow; he believed in chewing each piece of meat thirty-five times.

"How do you have anything left to chew?" Sara asked him one night. "The meat's gone before I can chew it that much."

"If you gabbed less, young lady, you could eat properly," he said.

"It's important to have conversation during dinner," I said. "It's our one chance of the day to be together."

Annie set down her fork. "I'm through with Peter. I just decided. This is absolutely the end."

"I'm sorry," I said. "He seemed so nice the day he came over and baked bread with you."

"He pretended to be the sensitive type, but deep down, he was no different than the rest. A real snake."

"What'd he do?" Sara wanted to know.

"Is this what you call conversation?" said my grandfather. "The pot roast is getting cold."

"I'll tell you everything later, in private," Annie told Sara and me.

"And you, stop slurping!" my grandfather said to Sara.

She looked surprised. "Grandpa, that's not slurping," she said. "This is slurping." She made a loud noise with her milk, and he reached over and slapped her cheek.

In an instant, Sara's head was pressed into my lap. "That was plain fresh," said my grandfather.

"I was just showing you," Sara sobbed.

"End of discussion," he said, putting a piece of meat in his mouth.

"No, it's not," I said. "That was uncalled-for. Sara was not being fresh. This is not your house. While you're here, you have to follow our rules, and no one gets slapped. Ever."

He swallowed and carefully tapped his lips with one of Charlotte's best linen napkins. Everyone else had been considerate enough not to use them. "Whose house is this?" he said. "That's an excellent question. You saw your chance. You walked right in here and took over, and now you think you can give the orders. Where's Sam? That's the person I'm sorry for. You walked in, took over his domain and —"

He hadn't chewed his last bite as meticulously as he usually did. All of a sudden, he coughed, turned red, and bent over his plate. You could see the space between his upper dentures and his gums. No one slapped him on the back. No one handed him a glass of water. We all just sat there and watched him choke.

Fortunately, Aunt Clara's stroke wasn't nearly as bad as everyone had feared. When the doctor said she could go home any day, my grandfather started looking for a private duty nurse to take care of her up at the lake.

My mother and I decided that it would be all right for Annie and Sara to visit Aunt Clara, and one Saturday morning, I drove them in to the city.

"This is a hospital we're going to," I reminded the girls on the way. "That means sick people. That means quiet."

"I know," said Sara. "I've been to a hospital before."

"That's a lie," Annie said.

"It is not."

"When?"

"When I was born."

"Like that really counts," said Annie.

"Aunt Lou, tell about the day I was born," Sara cried.

"It was the hottest day of the year. Our clothes were sticking to us, even in the shade. Your mother woke up feeling lucky."

"So you went to the racetrack," Sara said.

"She was so big, everyone was staring. Afterward we kept saying we should have known. She looked big enough to burst."

"How many times do I have to hear this boring story?" said Annie.

"You weren't there," said Sara. "You had to stay with Grandma and Grandpa because you were just a baby." She tugged my sleeve. "Tell about the man who bought drinks."

"He pushed his hat back on his forehead and laid his big paw right on top of your mother's belly," I said.

Sara shrieked. "So, did Mommy win?"

"Four hundred and fifty dollars."

"And what about you and Daddy?"

"Not a cent."

"And then Mommy fainted, and then you went to the hospital, and then I came!" Sara cried.

"That's right," I said. "Now look out for a parking space."

At the hospital in Saratoga, I'd sat in the waiting room down the hall from Charlotte's room at first, listening to her screams. But I decided it was worse not being able to see her, and I went and joined Sam by her bedside. I hadn't eaten since breakfast, and I was jittery from the cocktails at the racetrack and hospital coffee. A few times I had to sit down and hang my head between my knees. Near the end, the doctor said, "She's crowning, she's crowning," and in my confusion, I pictured *Queen for a Day* and my mother scorching one of my father's handkerchiefs with all the excitement.

Outside Aunt Clara's room, my mother was waiting for us. She'd driven my grandfather in earlier. He'd already visited with his sister and was down the hall, complaining to one of the nurses.

"Aunt Clara, here are the girls," said my mother, ushering us into the room.

The metal slats on Aunt Clara's bed were up. "Why's she in a crib?" Sara whispered.

Aunt Clara opened her eyes. In the pink satin bed jacket my mother had bought her, she seemed for the first time like a very old woman. Her eyes were dim and someone had curled her hair; before she'd always worn it straight. Her skin looked doughy, but when I bent to kiss her, it felt like a brown paper bag.

Aunt Clara stared at Annie. "Are you a girl or a boy?" she said.

"You know who Annie is, Aunt Clara," my mother said quickly, reaching over to fluff Annie's hair.

Sara giggled. Annie pulled away. She was tall and graceful, but her hair was as short as a marine's.

"Aunt Clara's not herself yet," I whispered.

"Charlotte, it's rude to whisper," Aunt Clara said, pointing a quivering finger at me.

"That's Lou, not Charlotte," my mother said.

"Where's the fat lady?" said Aunt Clara.

"That was Nora," my mother said. "That was yesterday."

"It's not nice to call Mrs. Lacey fat," Annie said.

"Fat's in the genes," Aunt Clara said. "Nothing you can do about it. Where's my purse?"

"It was right here beside you." My mother hunted under the bedclothes.

"Where's my purse!"

My mother picked it up from the floor. "Here," she said, tucking it next to Aunt Clara's skinny arm.

"*Where's my purse?*" Aunt Clara screamed.

"I think we've had enough company," said my mother.

I herded the girls out of the room. "Who'd want her damn purse?" Annie muttered.

"I thought she was going to give us some money," Sara said.

I led them down the hall to the waiting room. "Don't think of her like this," I said. "Remember her the way she was on Fourth of July."

"How could she think I'm a boy?" Annie said. She stuck out her chest. "I've got tits."

"She does, you know," Sara said.

"Aunt Clara didn't mean to hurt your feelings," I said.

"Where's my purse?" mimicked Annie. "*Where's my purse?*"

"Sit down," I said. "We have to wait for the others."

"What are genes?" Sara said.

"They're how your characteristics are passed to you from your parents, and how you'll pass them to your children. I forget exactly how it works. You'll learn about it in high school biology."

"Do you think fat is in my genes?" she asked.

"Yours is mostly baby fat," I said.

"But I'm not a baby anymore."

"Good point," said Annie.

"Everyone develops at her own rate," I said. "But you could try eating that melba toast I bought you, instead of cookies."

"I hate melba toast and I hate cottage cheese, too, for your information."

I didn't say anything.

"Aunt Lou?"

"Leave me alone a minute."

"How come?"

"Because I'm feeling sad."

"It was too much confusion," my mother said, coming into the waiting room with my grandfather a few minutes later.

"I can't for the life of me figure out who this confounded Milly is," my grandfather said.

"Are you sure she wasn't a neighbor?" I said. "Or one of Aunt Clara's school friends?"

"Who wants to eat lunch in the cafeteria?" My mother hooked her arms through Annie's and Sara's. "I haven't had lunch with my two favorite girls in a dog's age."

"How long's a dog's age?" Sara said as we all left the waiting room.

In the hospital cafeteria, we found a free table, and the girls went for trays. The rest of us weren't hungry. "It was too much confusion," my mother said again.

"She's getting worse," said my grandfather. "She was calling Lou Charlotte."

"That's an honest mistake," my mother said.

"Lou is nothing like Charlotte."

"Oh, Pop, just look at those eyes."

He stared at me. I struggled not to look away. "Maybe I'm the one who's confused," he finally said.

"It's going to be okay." My mother patted his shoulder.

"Please stop patting and pawing me," he said. "And stop saying okay. It's not a real word. I don't know why you use it. I don't know where it came from, but it's ruining the English language."

My mother folded her arms and looked away, but I leaned across the table toward him. "I know how you feel," I said. He looked up, ready to give it to me. He couldn't stand anyone thinking that they understood him. But instead of saying something nasty, he nodded. "I guess if anyone does, it's probably you, Louise." He took my hand and held it a moment; then he realized what he was doing and let go.

After days of interviews and hating every person he met, my grandfather hired a nurse, a Miss Rogers, who called him sir without being instructed to and wore a crisp white apron and cap. The morning of Aunt Clara's release from the hospital, my mother and I watched my grandfather walk slowly down the driveway with his suitcase toward the shiny blue van he'd rented to haul Aunt Clara and all her equipment home. At the nurse's advice, he'd also rented a hospital bed, a wheelchair, and a whirlpool device that fit in the bathtub.

"God knows, he's my father and I love him," said my mother. "But I'm glad to be getting rid of him."

A few hours later she and I were having lunch, when she suddenly jumped up and hurried to the window. "What're they doing back here?" she cried. I got up, too, and saw the blue van pulling into the driveway. "They were leaving straight from the hospital," my mother said. "They weren't planning to stop here."

"Grandpa probably forgot something," I said.

"I don't think I can face him again."

"Maybe Aunt Clara just wanted to say good-bye."

"Do you know what he told me last night? He's disappointed the way his family turned out. A babysitter and a short-order cook — that's how he described you and me."

Miss Rogers got out of the driver's seat and walked around to the other side of the van. Using a hydraulic lift, she lowered a wheelchair with Aunt Clara in it, then pushed it up the driveway toward the side porch of my mother's house. A red tartan overnight case lay across the arms of the chair with Aunt Clara's hands folded on top.

"Hello, Liz," Aunt Clara called, as my mother opened the kitchen door. "I think I'll do best on the pullout couch in the study, don't you?"

"It's not very comfortable," my mother said. "They told me it was a high-density foam, but I suspect it's just foam chips."

"Clara, don't be a damn fool," my grandfather shouted from the van.

Hearing his voice, the nurse paused. "Miss Rogers, stop gaping and kindly get her back in here," he said.

Miss Rogers hesitated. To someone unaccustomed to my grandfather, he must have sounded terrifying. "If I have to get myself up from this seat to straighten out this mess, everyone is going to be sorry," he bellowed.

"Kindly stop shouting," Aunt Clara said. "If you have something sensible to say, Charles, we'll listen, but not when you're using that tone of voice."

"I've said all there is to say," my grandfather said.

"He has, believe me," Miss Rogers muttered.

"What's going on?" my mother asked the nurse.

"Your aunt refuses to go back and live with her brother."

"I have the money from my AT&T shares, Liz, which I intend to contribute to your household," Aunt Clara announced.

From her purse, she took a bank book and held it toward my mother. "I can be a help around here," she said. "I'll be out of this donkey cart in a day or two, and I'll have my sea legs back in no time."

"I'm counting to ten!" my grandfather shouted.

Everyone was at a standstill, frozen in place. My mother was clearly struggling with her conscience. How could she say no to Aunt Clara, who'd been like a mother to her? But she was afraid of my grandfather.

The nurse reached down and checked Aunt Clara's pulse. "Aunt Clara, couldn't you try and talk to Grandpa?" I said. "Away from everyone. Just the two of you."

"Lou, I've been trying to talk to him since he was a baby in his cradle," she said. "Your grandfather was born mean.

He terrorized our mother. He put glue in my hair. He dragged cats by the tails. Then he met Sylvia. I thought, either this woman is deaf, dumb, and blind, or Charles is changing. But it was just an act. At my second wedding, he held up his champagne glass and said, 'Let's hope this is the last toast I have to make for Clara.' At my third wedding, he refused to make a toast. How was I supposed to feel? He's never shown me an ounce of human kindness, and I refuse to spend my last years with him."

When Aunt Clara had finished, my mother opened the door as wide as it would go. "What's the best way to get you in here?" she said.

"Well, if Miss Rogers will take one side, and Lou, the other, I think we can manage just fine," Aunt Clara said.

As the nurse and I got Aunt Clara and her wheelchair safely inside, my grandfather struggled out of the van. My mother and Miss Rogers went back outside, and Aunt Clara and I listened, breathless, by the door.

"Pop, you have gone too far," my mother said.

"I certainly have. I should have left her in the hospital. I should never have hired that fool nurse and that wheelchair, not to mention a truckload of expensive machinery. You're right, I've gone too far. Next time I'll leave her in the hospital to rot."

"I'd like to be released," Miss Rogers said.

"You're released," he snapped.

"I need to pass on my orders."

"Pass them on to me," my mother said.

"Elizabeth," my grandfather said softly. "I am not leaving Clara here."

"She'll be fine, Pop," my mother said. Miss Rogers pulled a set of stapled instructions from her bag.

"I'm not leaving her," my grandfather repeated, and with difficulty, lowered himself onto the steps.

At first my mother looked fed up, but then her expression softened. After all, this was what she admired most — families sticking together, no matter what.

fourteen

EVERY MORNING, my grandfather walked to the shopping center for the newspapers. He acted as if he was doing the others an enormous favor, but nobody read them except him. My mother and Aunt Clara listened to the news between talk shows. Usually, their interest was in stories that my grandfather thought inconsequential — fires in Newark, bus crashes in Baltimore. "Idiots," he muttered from time to time, but he didn't give any lectures.

Sitting at the piano, I would see him passing our house. I'd finally begun to practice again, first thing in the morning while the girls were getting ready for school. I had to get my fingers back in shape, and knowing someone was listening helped me begin. Annie said the music soothed her nerves, especially the Chopin. When she came home in the afternoon, she lay on the carpet, listening to me play the same phrases over and over again.

I practiced in the evening, too, after dinner, while the girls sat on the couch doing their homework. With Sam away in Japan, we didn't have his arrival to remind us that it was getting late, and sometimes it was eleven o'clock before the girls stumbled up to bed.

All the time that Sam was gone, the girls lived for his return. They seemed to have forgotten what their father was like, substituting a man who was warm and loving and always around. I knew the disappointment they were in for when they saw him again. I got my hopes up about people, too. For instance, I'd been certain that my father would remember my mother's birthday last month. It would have meant the world to her for something with his name attached to arrive, but nothing came, not a bushel of Florida oranges, not even a postcard, and I remembered that my father had always been impossible about birthdays. He could never keep the dates straight.

Then there was Richard. He refused to acknowledge that this was my life now. But why should that disappoint me? His stubbornness was one of the things that had drawn me to him in the first place.

As a surprise, the girls and I were picking Sam up from the airport. I'd been checking with his secretary every day for the last week of his trip to make sure he hadn't changed his travel plans.

On the way to the airport, the girls worked themselves into such a state of nervous excitement that when we got caught in a traffic jam, Sara started to cry. We finally arrived, only to find that the flight from Tokyo had been delayed three hours. There was nothing to do but wait. Annie and Sara ate candy bars, flipped through comic books and *Seventeen,* and made numerous expeditions to the ladies' room.

By the time Sam arrived, they were sick to their stomachs and bored. They greeted their father with a quick kiss and argued with each other all the way home in the car. Sam finally turned around and said, "What's gotten into you two?" That did it. At home, they were polite but cool when he presented them with kimonos of gold and magenta silk, luxurious robes whose value they couldn't begin to appreciate.

Despite all the measurements Sam had taken, the kimonos were big enough for someone my size, and I had to shorten the hems and sleeves and make tucks so they'd fit the girls. "Stand still," I told Sara, a few days before Halloween, as I pinned the hem of her robe. It was lunchtime, and she was in a flurry, searching for a book she wanted to lend her new best friend.

"If you don't find it now, you can always bring it to Ruth tomorrow," I said. "It'll show up. Turn around."

"But I promised," Sara said, whirling.

"Slow," I told her. "I want to make sure it's even."

When I was finished, she raced upstairs to continue her search. In minutes, she was back, empty-handed and frantic. "What if she won't be my best friend anymore? What if she picks someone else?"

"A real friend wouldn't do that."

"You don't understand!" Sara wailed, and took off again. I dropped the crusts of her sandwich in the garbage and rinsed her plate.

"Found it!" she cried, running in. "It was under the cushions on the couch. I forgot. I hid it so no one would steal it."

She stuffed a handful of candy corn into her mouth. Before she came home I'd been filling the trick or treat bags. "Ruth thinks my hair is gorgeous," she told me. "She says one time I can come over to her house and she'll curl it with her mother's electric rollers."

Soon after Sara left for school, my mother stopped by. "I'm late, I'm meeting Nora for lunch," she said, popping a piece of candy in her mouth. "What I should be doing is cleaning the house. With Pop and Aunt Clara, it's a mess. Pop walks around with a dust cloth to make me feel guilty, but he's never cleaned in his life."

"Are he and Aunt Clara speaking yet?" I asked.

My mother shook her head. "Not only that, but she refuses to eat at the same table with him. I make dinner before I leave for work, Aunt Clara takes hers into the den, and Pop sits at the dining room table alone, sulking. And his idea of doing dishes —"

"I should send Sara over. She's working on her housekeeping badge."

"I thought she quit Scouts," said my mother.

"One of the girls in her troop has an older brother with a motorcycle. Annie's paying Sara a quarter a week to stay in the Scouts till she figures out how to meet him. She actually picks Sara up after meetings."

"Oh, Lord." My mother smiled. "By the way, we finally figured out who Milly was — Pop and Aunt Clara's golden retriever when they were kids. Pop was fit to be tied."

I laughed.

My mother looked up at the clock, then back at me. "Did the girls say anything?"

I shook my head. It was a year that day since Charlotte died.

"Come have lunch with Nora and me," my mother offered.

"I still have these hems."

"I wish you'd get out more, sweetie. You could swim at the Y, you know. Fred just joined, Nora was telling me."

I'd gone to Fred and asked him what I should do for Charlotte that day. "Flowers for the grave," he told me right away. He didn't have to think. That was the good part about religion — having rituals to follow. It helped in other ways, too. It helped you not to worry that you could have done something. It taught you that everything happened for a reason.

Sometimes I imagined that I was there when the pumpkins started to fall. I was in the passenger seat of Charlotte's car, and I was ready. I grabbed the steering wheel and spun it, hand over hand, swerving the car out of the way, to safety.

When I called the florist, he had only carnations and gladioli and roses — hothouse flowers that Charlotte would have hated. "We won't get daffodils till March at the earliest," the florist said. "Can I interest you in a nice African violet?" In the end, I bought nothing.

That afternoon, I drove through the stone posts at the entrance to the cemetery and parked in the lot beside the caretaker's office. I climbed to the top of the hill on foot, where the columns of graves ended abruptly, and a field of laurel fell over the crest.

When I looked below, I could see the town, a wide main

street paralleling the river, with neighborhoods in neat blocks, separated by clumps of trees. At one time, the whole place had been a forest. Soon, what was left of it would be replaced by houses, and Nora had my mother convinced that the riverfront was going to be developed with high-rise apartment buildings and shops, but for now, the church steeple was the highest point around, and if an old woman was lucky, a stock boy at the market would help her home with her groceries. It wasn't a bad place to live.

When I turned around, Sam was walking toward Charlotte's tombstone, and I saw that he wasn't carrying anything. Either he hadn't known what to bring, or like me, he'd tried and decided on nothing, rather than something Charlotte wouldn't like. At the foot of the grave, he knelt and bowed his head.

Fred had told me that in certain cultures cemeteries were placed on the highest hill around, so that the dead were closer to heaven and it was easier for God to scoop them up. Fred knew a lot about religion, but some of the things that he told me seemed downright foolish.

"God has no idea what life is like down here," I once said.

"God *is* life down here," was Fred's firm reply.

While I watched Sam, the wind rustled down the hillside, taking some of the fallen leaves with it. I shivered and sunk my hands into the pockets of my sweater. Sometimes it seemed as if ten Charlottes had died.

Sam was still praying. I prayed, too, but never on purpose. Prayers came to me at odd times and odd places, like lonely strangers who dropped down beside you on the train, impossible to ignore. Sometimes when I couldn't sleep at night, the prayers I'd learned in catechism class passed through my lips, a reflex as strong as my heartbeat or the rise and fall of my lungs. The prayers formed pictures: Charlotte in her confirmation robe, looking like an altar boy except for the bobbing curls at her ears. Me in my white Holy Communion dress, hands folded, head bowed in front of a bed of blooming azaleas. Scapulars — two holy pictures mounted on felt, which hung from black ribbons on our backs and chests. Worn all day beneath our undershirts, they itched and ended up peaking out from our collars.

When Sam looked up and saw me, he waved and started climbing the hill, moving like an old man in the wind, stiff-backed and inflexible. He must have felt chilly wearing just a suit. I had on a sweater made of mountain goats' wool and boots from one of Fred's catalogues. Fred had been especially pleased when the boots arrived. "Vibram soles, fiberglass shanks, fully insulated and waterproofed," he said as he examined them. "They're lightweight too, won't weigh you down." Because it was easier than going shopping, I'd taken Fred's advice and looked through his fall catalogues. What I'd ended up with, though, was a wardrobe for a mountaineer, more suitable for Norway than New York in October.

"Sara had her kimono on at lunchtime," I told Sam when he dropped down beside me. "She looked adorable. Wait'll you see. I'll have her and Annie model tonight."

Sam nodded. "What do you think?" he said. "Should I get Annie a computer for Christmas, or not? Part of me thinks that whatever I buy her now will be outdated in a year, so why not wait till she's older, going off to college. The other part of me thinks that's no way to live, always waiting to make someone happy."

"She's been wanting a computer for a while now."

Just then, a car pulled up the hill, and Fred got out, opened the hatchback, and unloaded half a dozen pots of yellow mums. He set the pots on the grave, stood back to look, then rearranged them. For a good five minutes, he fiddled with them, moving them this way and that, until finally he was satisfied.

"What's he doing?" Sam asked.

"He likes to get things right."

A few minutes later, as Fred got back into his car, Sam said,

"I'm going to talk to my office manager tomorrow, see what he recommends."

"What?" Fred was leaving without having noticed Sam and me. He hadn't even looked up the hill.

"What kind of computer I should get," Sam said.

"What Annie wants more than any computer is to spend time with you."

Sam tilted his head. "I don't know what to say to the girls," he finally confessed.

"What makes you think I do?"

"Everything I say, they take wrong."

"You could try a little."

He stared back at the ground. "Nan has a way with them. They seem to really enjoy being with her."

I got up to leave. Sam still hadn't told me that he was seeing Nan Gordon. "All that curtsying and the Madame business get on my nerves," I said. Then I started down the hill alone.

When I arrived home, Annie was sitting at the kitchen table, reading brownie mix instructions out loud to Sara. "Beat an egg," she said.

Sara held up her cheek to be kissed, then broke an egg into a mixing bowl. "These aren't for us," she told me. "They're for the Girl Scout bake sale." She stabbed the yolk with the prongs of a fork.

"Not like that," Annie said. "Like this." She demonstrated, whisking the air.

But when Sara tried, the yolk just slid around the bowl, dragging the slimy gray white with it. Exasperated, she dropped the fork on the floor. I picked it up and rinsed it off. "Here, I'll show you," I said.

"Sara can do it." Annie gave me a look. She thought I babied Sara. "You make tea," she ordered me.

While I obediently opened the canister that held tea bags, Sara tried again to beat the egg, this time with more success. "Okay, now what?" she asked Annie.

"One quarter cup of water. Then mix with a wooden spoon. Fifty strokes, no more."

"Can't I use this one?" said Sara, holding up a stainless steel spoon.

"Absolutely not. What did I tell you about following directions exactly?"

Sara sighed and hunted in the drawer.

When the telephone rang, Annie jumped up, slicking her lips with her tongue. "I got it," she said, but she let the phone ring while she tucked her turtleneck into her jeans. When she finally picked up, she said, "Asher residence."

She listened, then cried, "We saw your picture in the paper! I cut it out and put it in my scrapbook." She listened again and started giggling. "Sure." She handed the phone to me, whispering, "Be nice."

"I just wanted you to know I'm thinking of you," Richard said. "Are you okay?"

I didn't say anything.

"Dumb question. Of course you're not. Remember: one way or another, Charlotte's always with you. I'm with you, too," he added. "One way or another."

Charlotte's hair had grown darker during her two pregnancies, and soon after Sara was born, she began streaking it. The day she died, she'd had an appointment to have her roots touched up.

When my mother arrived at the hospital that afternoon, the body was covered, but a strand of platinum blond hair had escaped the sheet. Seeing it, my mother breathed easy again. "That's not my daughter," she said.

Even when the nurse handed her Charlotte's wallet, my mother wouldn't believe it. She wouldn't believe it until she saw for herself that instead of her usual streaks, Charlotte had had her hair bleached that morning and looked like a total stranger.

I'd been gazing out the window of my classroom right around the time Charlotte must have turned onto Bridge

Street, where the crash occurred. It was an ungodly day, a sky too vivid, the leaves bloody and gold. It was a Wednesday. My father was playing his weekly eighteen holes. Once my mother learned what had happened, she left a message for him at the country club to call home as soon as he got in from the golf course. Then she called Sam, reaching him in the nick of time, before he went into a meeting. He took a cab to the hospital all the way from the city.

When Annie and Sara came home from school that afternoon, they wondered where their mother was, but they didn't worry. Charlotte had told them that if ever for some reason she wasn't there when they came in, they could have two cookies apiece.

"I'll tell the girls," Sam had said, as my mother drove up the driveway.

But when Annie asked what he was doing home so early, all he could say was, "Your mother, your mother," like a broken record.

Sara giggled, then looked scared. Finally, my mother took the girls into the kitchen and told them what had happened. Then she started supper. She tied aprons around the girls' middles. She gave Annie potatoes to peel, and Sara, carrots. She took a bowl of marinating stew meat from the refrigerator, then went into the den to try the country club again. My father was having a rum and Coke at the bar. He hadn't gotten her message.

After she told him, she called me. "I'm having a rotten day," I said, before she had a chance to say anything. "Can I call you later? I've still got two lessons, back to back. It's Wednesday."

"That's right," she said. "Your father played golf."

When my mother went back to the kitchen, the girls had disappeared. She threw the meat and vegetables into a stewpot and picked up the phone to call me again. But just then, the girls returned, and Annie explained that Sara had been afraid to go to the bathroom alone.

Someone had to drive into the city and tell me in person.

Not my mother — she couldn't leave the girls. Not my father — a doctor at the club had given him a Valium and he'd passed out on a couch in the lounge. My mother had no choice but to send Sam.

After Sam told me, I went into my bedroom and saw the onyx earring on the dresser. Charlotte had its mate. They were hers. The last time she'd been over, this one had fallen from her ear.

When Sam came in from the cemetery, he made a big effort, calling out, "Hi, kids!" He must have taken my words to heart.

But Annie said, "We're not young goats."

"Excuse me. Hi, young ladies." Sam sat down beside Annie and watched her leaf through an early Christmas catalogue that had come in the mail. I was standing at the stove. I'd put water on to boil.

Annie pointed to something red at the top of the page and said, "That would look good on me. Is Santa Claus listening?"

"He's listening," Sam said.

"Aunt Lou, look!"

"Hmmmm?"

"Aunt Lou," said Annie. "A watched pot never boils."

Charlotte and I had been raised on maxims like that. Waste not, want not. A bird in the hand is worth two in the bush. Don't let the sun go down on your anger. That last one meant that even if Charlotte and I were mad at each other, we had to find a way to patch things up before we went to sleep.

Sam cleared his throat. "Lou?"

Instead of pouring the boiling water into the teapot, I'd emptied the kettle down the drain. When I turned around, the girls were staring at me with funny expressions. "Are you okay?" Sam said.

"I was daydreaming."

"Hello, everyone!" Fred called, coming in without knocking, already half out of his jacket. He kissed Sara and Annie and me, moving through the room with his cold lips and fresh smell. He pounded Sam on the shoulder.

"Watch this," he said, taking a scissors from the hardware drawer. By now, he knew where everything was kept. He sat beside Sam and flipped through the catalogue. He cut out three forms, then snipped them in pieces. As he reassembled them, the girls giggled — a baby in a strapless evening gown and basketball sneakers, a blonde with a hairy chest and chubby baby legs.

"Fred's funny, isn't he, Daddy?" Sara said.

Sam nodded. "Very funny."

Who knew what Sam was thinking then, watching his daughters laugh? I made assumptions about him. I assumed his grief was endless. I assumed his reticence with the girls and me had to do with his desire not to be reminded by a look or a gesture or a phrase of Charlotte.

He might have been wondering now if the girls remembered what day it was. He might have wanted to tell them. He might have been annoyed at Fred for knowing how to make them laugh, so easily and so hard. Or maybe Sam wasn't thinking about the girls at all. Maybe he was remembering the first time he'd set eyes on Charlotte, the first time she fell asleep beside him, the feel of her leg against his. But there was another possibility. Maybe he wasn't thinking about Charlotte or the girls. Maybe his thoughts were next door.

fifteen

THE BRIGHT AUTUMN weather ended without warning one day, and the sky turned a dismal gray. It happened with the same abruptness every November, but each year I had to get used to it all over again. I didn't do chores or practice the Rachmaninoff concerto I was working on. I moped around, not getting anything done.

Sara arrived home at noon starving, and I didn't have her lunch ready. "The morning flew by" was my excuse, and she pouted as I searched in the refrigerator.

"What were you doing?" she asked me.

"Nothing."

"Then how come you forgot about me?"

"I didn't forget about you. What about an omelette?"

"I had egg salad yesterday," Sara said.

I opened the cupboard and took out a can of tuna fish, but Sara vehemently shook her head. "Isn't it enough that we're living in the middle of a cancer zone?" she said. "Isn't it enough that I'm breathing polluted air twenty-four hours a day?"

Her class had just completed a science unit called "Cancer and You." Every day she came home with more things she'd never eat again. Tuna. Peanut butter. Apples. She'd warned me that next summer I couldn't use lighter fluid to start fires in the grill, and no bug spray, either.

"I'm no expert," I said. "But I know you're not going to die from one little tuna fish sandwich."

"Forget it. I'm not hungry."

"If you don't eat something, your stomach's going to growl all afternoon." I opened the refrigerator again.

"What about that?" Sara said, pointing to a brown-wrapped package.

"You won't like that."

"Yuck," said Sara, when she unfolded the paper and found a stack of hard salami. "Why'd you buy this stuff?"

"I suddenly had a craving." I rolled a slice of salami into a tube and dabbed it in a jar of mustard.

"What's a craving?" asked Sara.

"It's when you suddenly can't live without something." I handed her a slice. "Try it."

"What are the little white spots?" she asked.

"Don't look, just eat."

"Wait a minute. This is like bacon, isn't it? Nitrites?" She shook her head and handed the salami back to me.

I sighed. "Raisin bran, then. Bran prevents cancer, doesn't it?"

"People don't eat cereal for lunch," Sara said. "I'm telling Daddy you're neglecting me."

"Here." I put her jacket over her shoulders.

"Where're we going?"

"You're going to Grandma's. She'll make you lunch."

Sara put her hands on her hips. "Are you going to leave us?"

"Leave you?"

"You're not going to disappear?"

"Where would I disappear to?"

She turned and started for the door, then stopped. "You come with me," she said.

When we got to my mother's she had just finished making a platter of turkey sandwiches, and she handed one to Sara.

"Come sit here, sweetheart," Aunt Clara said, patting the chair beside her.

"That's my place," said my grandfather.

Aunt Clara ignored him.

"Pop, sit here, next to Lou," said my mother. "Sara, what did you do in school this morning?"

"Arithmetic, science, and sex education," Sara said.

"What about a pickle with that sandwich? Would you like a pickle?"

"Only if it's a dill."

"I'm pretty sure they're dill," my mother said, going to the refrigerator.

"Did I hear correctly?" said my grandfather. "Did I hear you correctly, Sara?"

"I only like dill ones," she said.

"Arithmetic, science, and what?"

"Sex education. Last year it used to be called health, and they talked about brushing your teeth."

"Who wants another sandwich?" said my mother. "More iced tea? Aunt Clara, are you okay over there?"

"Am I alone in being horrified and dismayed?" said my grandfather.

"Yes, Charles, as usual, you're alone," Aunt Clara said. "Now hush up. It's not often I'm lucky enough to have lunch with Sara."

"I've half a mind to write a letter to the school board."

"Oh, Pop, it's better they learn at school than on the street," said my mother.

"What's wrong with sex education?" Sara said.

"Certain subjects belong behind closed doors," he told her.

"It's reverse psychology, Grandpa," she said. "They figure if they tell us all about sex, we'll lose interest."

My grandfather choked on his tea. "If there's anything you want to know, just ask me," Sara added. "I'm probably getting an A."

My mother glanced at me. "Sara," I said. "Eat."

She stuffed the last bite of sandwich in her mouth. "I'm done."

"Be quiet and chew," I told her.

But with her mouth full, she twisted around to Aunt Clara and said, "Why did you get married so many times?"

"Good question," muttered my grandfather.

"No, it's not a good question," Aunt Clara said. "The good question is why didn't my first two marriages work. I thought I loved Martin and I thought I loved Reg. I was happy with both of them — for a while, anyway. Was it my fault? Was I too hasty? Why didn't I just wait for John? But I never would have met John if I hadn't married Martin. And maybe if John hadn't died, things would have gone downhill with him, too."

"Sara, how about an apple?" said my mother.

"I think about my husbands, you know," Aunt Clara said. She pushed away from the table and stood up. She hadn't recovered her sureness since the stroke. My mother had bought her a pair of sneakers, but Aunt Clara couldn't get used to them. She stepped gingerly with her plate and glass toward the sink.

"Do you think Daddy's ever going to get married again?" Sara asked.

"That, we don't know," my mother said.

"My guess is yes," said Aunt Clara.

Sara thought a moment, then turned to my grandfather. "How come you didn't get married again?"

"Sara, that's enough," my mother said.

"Can't I ask a question?"

"You know better than that," I said. "Some things are private."

"But Mommy said to ask if I don't understand. I don't see why Grandpa can't just tell me."

"If he doesn't want to tell you, he doesn't have to," said my mother. "Leave him be."

"We're not all like your mother, Sara," Aunt Clara said.

"For heaven's sake!" said my grandfather. "Give a person a chance. I fully intend to answer your question, Sara. I was just wondering what was the best way to express my feelings.

I didn't remarry because I didn't want to find out the hard way that certain things only happen once."

When I got home after dropping Sara off at school, Nan Gordon was in her backyard. It was windy and the tassels of her muffler whipped her cheeks as she lugged a sack of birdseed from feeder to feeder. There were six of them, I'd figured out, tucked beneath branches, camouflaged by bark, unnoticeable unless you knew where to look.

I didn't call out to Nan, or wave, and if she saw me, she pretended not to. Since our fight in the garden, we hadn't spoken, and Nan hadn't asked me to play piano for her ballet classes this year. If we met in the driveway and the girls were around we were civil, but when it was just the two of us, we both looked away.

I went on inside but watched Nan a moment longer through the kitchen window. After filling the last of the bird feeders, she sat down on a picnic bench and held out her palm. Did she really think the birds were going to eat from her hand? She sat there, like a statue.

I went into the living room and picked up *War and Peace*. After all these years, I still hadn't gotten through it. I was starting over again with a brand-new paperback copy. This time I was focusing on the love stories, not the war.

I opened the book, but moments later closed it and went into the kitchen for something to drink. "Why torture yourself?" Richard used to say, watching me start *War and Peace* again and again. "Everyone has a book they can't read. Look at me — I've never read *David Copperfield*."

"Dickens isn't nearly as great as Tolstoy," I said.

"Say you've read it," Richard suggested. "I'll never give you away."

But I couldn't do that.

I was watching out the kitchen window again when a large black bird landed on Nan's shoulder. If I'd been Nan, I'd have been afraid. What was to keep it from pecking her eyes out, or pulling hair from her head to make its nest? But then Nan raised her arm to form a bridge from her shoulder to her hand. The bird inched along. Nan's arm didn't waver; the bird never faltered. When it reached her wrist, protruding pale and sharp between her parka sleeve and her glove, it bowed its tiny head and ate.

"I just have a feeling — a premonition, you could call it," my mother said one morning the week before Thanksgiving. The two of us were in her kitchen planning the holiday dinner.

"But did he actually say he was coming home?" I asked.

"It wasn't what he said, it was his tone of voice. Your father always loved Thanksgiving. He thinks Christmas is too commercialized. With him, that makes eight," she said, jotting something down on a piece of paper. "I better call and tell the butcher I need a bigger bird."

"Don't expect him till you see the whites of his eyes," I said.

"Why do you have to burst my balloon?" my mother complained.

"I don't want you to be disappointed."

"Oh, Lou," she said sadly. "You've become so distrustful. But really, even when you were a baby, you used to stare up at me when I was diapering you, like I was about to do something wrong."

She went back to her list. "I want us to have happy holidays," she said. "I'm working on Pop and Aunt Clara. I told her he wanted to apologize, and I told him she wanted to apologize. I'm waiting to see what happens."

"I don't think you can count on Dad," I said.

"Your father sees his mistake. It happens, you know. And it's time you saw yours. Fred Lacey is not just a brainy little fat boy anymore."

"Mom —"

"No. For once, I'm going to say what I think. You deny yourself. It's true. I never should have let you move out here. The day you told me you were going to, I was overwhelmed.

I didn't see how I could cope all by myself. I was thinking of me, not you. It wasn't fair."

As a rule, my family communicated the way schoolboys do, tugging the pigtails of the people we loved. It was understandable that while my mother was speaking forthrightly, I wished a trap door would open beneath me. I was relieved to hear footsteps, first overhead, then coming down the back stairway.

"It's Pop," my mother said. "We'll continue this later."

I shook my head. "The subject is closed."

My mother and I both sat up straighter as my grandfather descended, his footsteps hesitant but heavy. "Elizabeth," he said from the doorway.

"Hi, Pop. Want some coffee? I made a fresh pot."

"What do you think coffee would do to my digestion?" he said. "Think about it."

"You worry too much about your digestion. I'm sure you could sit down and have a nice cup of coffee with Lou and me and feel just fine."

"Idiocy. Pure idiocy," he said. "Elizabeth, someone has been using my razor."

"The sterling silver one? It's so lovely."

"Elizabeth, this is not a girls' dormitory. I expect you to respect my privacy. All the things I can say about Clara, but one thing is certain — she knows better than to use my razor."

My mother turned to me. "I thought I'd try a chestnut stuffing this year. I found a recipe in *Gourmet*."

"I'm not finished!" said her father.

"What, then?"

For once, he didn't have an answer. He shuffled around the kitchen while my mother went through the menu she'd planned for Thanksgiving and we decided who would make what. She was planning a feast. "And dinner rolls," she finished. "We don't really need them, but Phillip likes a bit of bread with dinner."

"Phillip?" said my grandfather, turning toward us. "Did you say Phillip?"

"Yes."

"Do I understand you correctly? Is Phillip coming home for Thanksgiving?"

"It's looking more and more like it," my mother said.

"Does Clara know?"

"I haven't had a chance to tell her about this latest phone call," my mother said.

"If Phillip's coming, she'll want to go home. She won't want to intrude. I better get myself packed," my grandfather said, and he hurried out of the room.

My grandfather's cordovan suitcase stood ready and waiting at the head of the stairs until the Sunday after Thanksgiving, when he grudgingly dragged it back into his room. "Don't you dare say a word to Liz about Phil," Aunt Clara commanded him, and for once my grandfather kept his mouth shut.

When it had become clear that my father was not going to show up for Thanksgiving dinner, my mother, determined to fill the place she'd set for him, had phoned around, but everyone she tried was already busy. Jack had to work at the restaurant. Nora and Fred were visiting a distant relative in Philadelphia. My mother had even asked me if Richard might like to come. The answer to that was absolutely not. Finally, without consulting me, she invited Nan Gordon.

Thanksgiving night, after Sam and the girls and I had gone home, my mother telephoned me. "What's going on between Sam and Nan?"

Sam had played host that day, carving the turkey, keeping the wine glasses filled, listening to my grandfather's complaints. He'd smiled a lot, his cheeks rosy. You'd have to be blind not to have noticed how often he brushed against Nan's shoulder. When he wasn't beside her, his eyes were on her. She was like a magnet for him, in a red dress and heels, instead of her usual dark sweaters and corduroys.

"Sam hasn't confided in me," I told my mother.

"Well, he likes her, that's obvious," my mother said. "And

she likes him. Lou, I know Nan's not the easiest person to get along with, but she's not a bad person and she was a friend of your sister's. I want you to make up with her. You two could be some comfort to each other."

When I didn't answer, she said, "Be a good girl and think about it. Now, let me go. I've got a mess to clean up here."

"I thought we had things pretty much cleaned up by the time I left."

"Oh, Pop was helping me empty the dishwasher, and he dropped the gravy boat. Not the good china one, thank God, but I hollered at him to get out, and now I've got to clean up the pieces and go apologize. So I guess I've got two messes to clean up." She laughed. "Pop and Aunt Clara are inside watching a Lawrence Welk special. Lawrence Welk — doesn't that take you back? Remember those sisters? What was their name? Do you think they were really sisters? I always had my doubts. You never could tell what they looked like, they had on so much makeup. I'm sure their hair was dyed."

"It never occurred to me that they weren't real sisters," I said.

"Oh, to be young and gullible," she said. "What siblings would sing corny songs together on the Lawrence Welk show? Picture Pop and Aunt Clara. Pop could play the uku-lele. Can't you see it — Pop with a ukulele on the Lawrence Welk show?"

I laughed.

"By the way," said my mother. "Thank you for not saying I told you so."

/ixteeN

"I CAN'T POSSIBLY accept this," I told Fred a few nights later, holding out the envelope that had arrived in the mail that afternoon. In it was a round-trip ticket to St. Martin.

"It's an early Christmas present," Fred said, pulling the belt of his bathrobe tighter. We were standing in the doorway of his house. It was only nine o'clock but beneath my coat, I had my nightgown tucked into my jeans. Since the mail arrived, I'd been trying to figure out what to say to Fred.

"I'm giving it to you early so you'll have time to get ready," he said. "Buy yourself a new bikini."

"I hope this ticket's refundable," I said.

"Don't worry. I've cleared it with Sam and your mother," Fred said. "It's okay with them. They can handle the girls for a week."

"It's not a question of Sam or my mother or the girls," I said. "It's a question of me."

Fred balanced a moment on one foot. "I guess I'm being too subtle," he said.

"There's nothing subtle about a ticket to the Caribbean."

He dropped to his knees in the hallway, landing with a thud.

"What're you doing?" I tugged his shoulders. "Get up."

"I love you." He clutched my legs. I tried to escape, but he was too strong for me.

"Let go!" I swatted his back.

He stood up and took my hands in his. "What I'm trying to say is I can't live without you."

"You can't decide that out of the blue," I said.

"Out of the blue?" For a moment, he looked hurt, and I was glad I hadn't said the first thing to cross my mind — that he was mistaken, he didn't love me, he loved Charlotte. "The moment I saw you, at the ice cream shop with Sara and your mother, I knew something like this was going to happen," he went on. "Didn't you? Didn't you feel something out of the ordinary that day?"

What had I been feeling that day? That it would be nice to have someone to talk to. I shivered and pulled my coat tighter around me.

"You're cold, come in," Fred said, holding open the door.

"I've got to get back. I left the girls alone. Sam's working late tonight."

"Promise you'll think about it," Fred said, and he kissed me.

That night, I had a hard time falling asleep. I couldn't just laugh off Fred's declaration the way I might have a few months ago. I'd grown to depend on him, no doubt about it.

I slept through my alarm the next morning and woke with a start. When I came down, Sam was sitting on the front stairs, Sara between his knees, brushing her hair. "You don't mean to tell me Aunt Lou does this every single morning?" he said.

"How am I supposed to?" Sara said. "It's too far to reach."

Looking at her, I thought of Fred cutting bodies out of the department store catalogue and reassembling them all wrong. Sara's hair was tiger-striped, halfway down her back, too voluptuous for her stocky little body.

"If you pulled it around to the front like this, you could do it yourself," Sam said.

"But I don't want to do it myself."

"Morning." I edged past them.

"I'm practicing for when you go away," Sam told me.

"What do you mean?" I said. "I'm not going anywhere."

"You see?" Sara said to Sam.

"What is this?" I said. "Everybody talking behind my back." I reached to take the brush from Sam. "I'll finish that."

But he put the brush down on the step beside him and deftly twisted Sara's hair into a braid. "I'm almost done."

"Daddy, how come you know how to braid?" Sara asked.

"When I was in college, my hair was practically as long as yours."

"It was?"

"You've seen the pictures," he said.

"I have?"

"Of course you have."

"I don't remember," Sara said.

"I'll pull them out this weekend," he told her. "They're in one of the photo albums."

"Maybe I did get a concussion when I fell off my bike last week," Sara said. "I'm starting not to remember anything."

"You only think you forget," Sam said. "I can help you remember. You just have to picture it. Remember the time the sparrow got caught in the chimney and your mother opened the flue and the bird came into the living room? We chased it all over the place, remember? And remember how she finally caught it?"

"With your hat," Sara said. "She dropped your hat on top of it."

"And remember what she said?"

Sara covered her ears and ran up the stairs.

"What did I do?" said Sam.

"Nothing." I picked up the brush and sat down to fix my own hair.

"Did I say something wrong?"

"No."

"Are you sure?" he asked.

"Sometimes they like to hear about Charlotte, sometimes they don't."

"I want you to tell me if you ever hear me say something wrong," he said.

"Fine."

He sat on the step above me and began braiding my hair. "I'm not going away with Fred," I said.

Sam freed a few strands of hair that were caught beneath my turtleneck. "It was presumptuous of him to think he could arrange a trip like that and consult everybody but me," I went on.

"It was romantic," said Sam.

"If only."

"I thought you liked Fred."

"Liking is one thing. Taking a trip is something else. He just assumed I'd go. You all assumed."

"Why wouldn't we?" said Sam. "He's over all the time. Do you have a thingamajig?" He'd finished braiding and needed to secure the end.

I fished in my pocket for an elastic.

"By the way," Sam said. "There's something I want to tell you."

I turned to face him.

"I've told them at the office I'm not going to be working late like I have been. I'm going to be spending a lot more time right here." Sam patted the step he was sitting on.

"Fine," I said, relieved to hear that was all he had to tell me.

"I just wanted you to know."

I stood up and started for the kitchen to fix breakfast. But then I stopped. "What did she say?" I asked Sam.

"Who?"

"Charlotte, when she caught the sparrow."

Sam smiled. "A bird in the hat is worth two in the flue."

Late that afternoon, a blizzard started up. The girls sat and watched the snow through the big living room window, their hands cupped around their eyes. When they turned back to the room, their eyes were glazed, and I knew from having done the same thing that what they were seeing now were snowflakes falling inside, too.

The snow was still coming down the next morning, and schools were closed. Sam set out for the train station in his ski jacket and hiking boots, but along the way he must have changed his mind. When the girls caught sight of him trudging back down the center of the road where the town snowplow had cleared a path, they could hardly contain themselves. In their nightgowns, they danced around the kitchen doing grand jetés and pirouettes, bumping into each other and not caring.

But before he reached our driveway, Sam turned up Nan Gordon's front walk. It was already shoveled, as if she'd been expecting him. The girls watched silently while their father disappeared inside Nan's house.

"It's a good thing I bought a new thing of Nestlé's Quik yesterday," I said. "Who wants cocoa?"

But the girls ignored me. I watched Annie trying to make sense of what was happening. Sara fidgeted.

"I like Nan, don't you?" she said to Annie.

"That's not the point," Annie said.

"I don't think you two should blow this out of proportion," I told them.

"Maybe he'll come home soon," Sara said hopefully.

While Annie and Sara went upstairs to get dressed, I started a fire. Soon we were settled in, Annie and Sara with their library books, me with my knitting. The steady clicking of the needles was like a train on its track, and the girls seemed to calm down. I was making sweaters for them. As soon as I finished the left sleeve on Sara's, I'd start Annie's.

At one time, I used to knit a lot — an afghan for Mrs. Rapetti, a scarf for Richard, matching mittens and tassel caps for the girls. I'd learned how to knit when Annie was born. For her, I made bonnets that were too big, bonnets that were too small, a fuzzy yellow sweater with sleeves long enough for a gorilla. Charlotte dutifully dressed the baby in my failures.

When Annie was born, the family went overboard. Aunt Clara ordered a layette from Saks Fifth Avenue. My grandfather, who never liked to part with anything, bought the baby a savings bond. Without knowing a thing about carpentry, my father began building Annie a Victorian dollhouse that took him nearly four years to complete.

When the dollhouse finally arrived, Annie and I sat in front of it and she gave me a tour. "This is the mommy and daddy's room. This is the girl's room. She has a real canopy bed."

"And where does the aunt sleep?" I asked her. "Here?"

"That's the boy's room," Annie said. "There's no room for the aunt."

"Well, she can sleep on the couch in the living room, can't she?"

Annie had looked up, shaking her head. "Aunt Lou," she said. "There's no aunt doll."

Midmorning, the telephone rang and Annie and Sara raced to answer it. It was only my mother, checking in, but she broke the spell, and the girls left me alone in the living room and wandered through the house. I heard doors opening and closing and water running and their voices, sometimes closer, sometimes farther away. As I knit, I braced myself for a fight erupting between them, but miraculously, they stayed friends.

Eventually, they returned to the living room with a shoebox of old snapshots. Ever since Sara found the box in the attic, they'd been quizzing me about those pictures.

"When was this?" Sara asked, holding one up for me to see.

"Camp," I told her, after glancing at the photograph for a moment. That summer Charlotte had grown three inches, seemingly overnight. In the picture, she was beaming, while I stood teary and squat beside her. I'd been homesick the entire month we were away.

Annie looked at the picture. "Maybe I should go to sleep-away camp."

"Why?" Sara said.

"Maybe I'd like it."

"Your mother loved camp," I said.

"But you hated it," Sara reminded me.

"Oh, I didn't really hate it."

"Don't lie. We can see." She pointed to my face in the snapshot.

"I think I'd like it," Annie said.

"Do you think I would?" Sara looked worried.

"You'd definitely hate it," Annie told her. "At camp, they make you get up early, when the sun comes up, and you have to eat at big tables with lots of people."

"Think about it," I said to them. "If you want, I can send away for some brochures."

"What if I went to camp and I hated it?" Sara said.

"Then I'd come get you."

"But all the other kids would think I was a baby."

"Let them think what they want to think."

"Do you want us to go?" Sara asked me.

I remembered last spring when it had crossed my mind to send them away. "I'd miss you like crazy."

Around lunchtime, the doorbell rang. "I'll get it," Sara shouted.

"I'm already here!" Annie sprinted ahead.

A gust of cold blew into the room and the flames of the fire quivered. "Who is it?" I called.

No one answered, and I was putting my knitting down carefully so I wouldn't drop a stitch, when I felt two hands cover my eyes. I knew right away who it was.

"Hi, Richard," I said.

He let go and flopped down beside me. "Surprise."

"How'd you get here?"

"I walked from the station."

Charlotte would have had a fit if she'd seen him, making a puddle on her damask couch. I led Richard into the hallway. There he handed me one garment after another — scarf, gloves, cap, parka, sweater. When he was stripped down, Richard turned to the girls and said, "I woke up craving a game of Monopoly."

He'd hardly finished saying the word, and the girls had run to fetch the Monopoly board from their room. While they were gone, Richard wound his finger in a lock of my hair. I closed my eyes. I forgot about the girls. I forgot about Sam and Nan. It was always that way. With Richard around, I could forget to breathe.

Everyone had a different strategy for winning Monopoly. I bought only prime properties; I liked to wipe out my opponents in a single blow, loading four hotels on Park Place. Annie hummed to distract us. Sara closed her eyes before rolling the dice and shouted, "Snake eyes!" She was incredibly lucky; she almost always landed on Go.

The girls watched Richard closely to see what his tactic would be. He didn't insist on a lucky marker the way Sara did. He didn't care who was banker. He didn't talk too much or too little, or bring up odd subjects to get your mind off the game.

The girls kept having to remind me that it was my turn or that I'd landed on one of their properties. When we took a break and I was in the kitchen making sandwiches and hot chocolate, I heard Sara say, "What's wrong with Aunt Lou?"

"She's happy to see Richard, that's what's wrong," Annie said.

An hour later, Richard won, and the girls got quiet. Except for their mother, they'd never met an adult who didn't go to great pains to make sure to lose when playing with kids.

"Great game," Richard said, not realizing he'd done anything out of the ordinary. He looked at his watch. "Good God! How'd it get so late?" He stood up.

"Do you have to go?" Sara said.

He tugged her braid. "I'm expecting some phone calls from California."

"Call from here," Annie suggested. "You can use Daddy's study. We'll keep quiet."

But Richard said, "I really have to go."

Sara sulked and refused to say good-bye, and Annie stuck

her head in her book. I bundled myself up and walked out with Richard.

"They hate for anyone to leave," I explained.

My hand was in his pocket, and he squeezed it. "They're sweet kids," he said.

That was all. Not, Come with me. Not, I can't live another second without you. Once he'd kissed me good-bye and set off down the street, Richard didn't look back. It was me who kept waving until he was out of sight.

Back inside, Sara was asking Annie, "So, you still really like him?"

"I already told you so. Quit pestering. I'm trying to read."

"Do you like him better than Fred?" Sara said, but Annie refused to look up from her book.

Sara watched for a minute, then said softly, "I saw you take two hundred dollar bills from the bank when you were pretending to be fixing the piles."

Annie turned red. She'd been known to cheat when she was younger, but we thought she'd outgrown that. "Take that back," she said.

"I saw," Sara insisted.

"You shut up!"

"You should be thanking me," Sara said. "You would have been embarrassed if I told in front of Richard."

Annie stood up, lifted her hand, and brought it down hard on Sara's shoulder. Sara staggered. Annie hit her again. I didn't move. It was a silent, dirty fight, and I did nothing to stop it. The girls bumped into a side table; a lamp crashed. They grunted and heaved, like wrestlers.

As the lamp fell, the front door opened and Sam came in. "What the heck is going on?" he cried, running over to separate Annie and Sara.

They were panting, crimson, unable to speak. But I knew what each one of them was feeling at that moment — the burning desire to hurl the other off the face of the earth.

·   ·   ·

The sun came out the next morning, and with all the snow on the ground, the light was blinding. School was still closed, and even though he could have returned to work, Sam stayed home again, this time out of guilt. After he'd sent the girls upstairs the day before, I told him we'd seen him go into Nan's house.

At breakfast, the girls still weren't speaking to each other. "I am deeply and eternally furious with Sara," Annie had said, and she'd slept in her sleeping bag on the floor of my room rather than breathe the same air as her sister. Neither of them would so much as look at their father.

Sam tried to get their attention. "Last week at the dentist's office, I read an article about ice fishing," he announced. "Imagine it — whole communities build little huts on the ice and fish all winter long. The article said it gets so hot inside that the fishermen have to take their shirts off."

Before he'd finished talking, Annie got up and carried her bowl over to the sink. She held it under the faucet and ran the water hard, until the remains of her oatmeal had disappeared down the drain.

"That's on Lake Ontario," Sam went on. "One of the Great Lakes. Have you studied the Great Lakes in geography yet?"

No one answered. Before Sara would think to ask for more, I threw the last spoonfuls of oatmeal into the garbage. "It looks like a perfect day for sledding," I said in my most cheerful voice.

"I hate my sled," Sara said.

"What's wrong with it?" I asked her.

"It's her old one. Why can't I ever have anything new? I always get hand-me-downs. I wish I had a saucer, instead."

"We'll get you one," Sam said. "We'll go out right now and get you one."

But she still refused to acknowledge him, and all of a sudden, I'd had it. "If you're mad at your father, why don't you say so?" I told her. "You're getting nowhere this way."

Sam looked down at his coffee cup.

"What you're forgetting, both of you," I went on, "is your father lost somebody, too. He feels just as lonely as you do."

After a silence that I thought would last forever, Annie said, "But you shouldn't have sneaked."

"You're right," Sam said. "I'm sorry."

"You treat me like I'm a kid," she went on.

"But we're not kids," said Sara.

Annie looked at her. "You are."

"I forget how grown up you're both getting," Sam said. "To me, you're my little girls."

I slipped out of the room, put on my coat, and left by the front door. No one called after me, "Stay." Nobody seemed to notice I'd gone.

I was tramping through the snow when I heard someone cry, "Ahoy there!"

I recognized Fred's voice before I recognized him. "What are you wearing?" I said, when he caught up with me.

"I am totally warm and dry," he said. "My equipment is a success."

Fred was double his normal size, in layers of thirty-below gear. "Where're you off to?" he asked, lifting his ski goggles and peeling up his face mask.

"Nowhere in particular."

"Let's go to the diner. I want flapjacks and bacon and maple syrup."

The diner was out past Our Lady of Miracles, past the housing developments that had gone up when Fred and I were kids. Now they blended in with the older neighborhoods like ours. The aluminum siding didn't seem as shiny, and the trees had finally grown above the rooftops.

By the time we reached the door to the diner, Fred's face was bright red. Bonnie hurried over to us. "Fred Lacey, don't come any further in those boots. I just got through mopping. Manny will make me do it all over again, if you mess up the floor. Take those things off right here."

He bent to undo the buckles, but couldn't reach, so Bonnie brought him a chair. Once he was seated, Fred unwound his scarf and pulled his face mask over his head. He unzipped his jacket, took off his boots, unfastened the clasps of his snow overalls and tucked them into his waist. Under the arms of his turtleneck were wet rings the size of melons. Fred's natural expression was a smile, but sometimes he smiled on top of that. "I am totally warm and dry," he said again, as he padded in his thick red socks over to a booth. "Pancakes," he cried. "Pancakes for everyone."

"You two are the only ones here," Bonnie pointed out.

"You're here," said Fred. "Manny's here."

"I'm on a diet, and Manny hates diner food."

"Pancakes for two, then," Fred said grandly.

"And two coffees, regular?" Bonnie said, scribbling in her order pad.

"Right." Fred grinned at me.

"What are you so happy about?" I asked.

"I was up all night with my book. I'm really close to being finished, I think."

"That's great," I said.

"Something occurred to me," Fred went on. "It's so obvious I can't believe I didn't think of it before. I started thinking about how I exercise my will, how I make choices. For example, why did I decide to take a walk on a freezing cold morning like this?"

"You were feeling cooped up?" I guessed.

He shook his head. "Because my image of myself is a guy who braves the elements. Why do I have all these clothes? Because part of the way I see myself is as an explorer. I didn't particularly want to leave my bed this morning, but when I looked out the window, I knew I belonged out here, and I had to be true to this picture of myself.

"What I'm saying," he went on, leaning his elbows on the table, "at least what I think I'm saying, is that there's no way we can respond only to the immediate situation. We respond to our entire lives reflected in the moment."

Bonnie set cups of coffee in front of Fred and me. "What are you ranting and raving about?" she said. "We could hear you all the way back in the kitchen."

"Sorry," said Fred.

"So what do you think?" he asked me after Bonnie had gone.

I was thinking back to the day I'd decided to move to Charlotte's. My mother's face had been grim and set. I tried to recall what had made me open my mouth.

"You're probably right," I finally said to Fred.

"It makes sense, doesn't it? That's why no one ever really changes. Who do you see when you look at me? I'm the same kid doing science experiments and wanting more ice cream. You're the same little girl trying to be like your big sister. We do what we do now because of the way we were when we were kids."

Bonnie returned with our stacks of pancakes. "Manny made them soft the way you like them, Fred," she said. "Lou, if they're too gooey for you, just holler." She bustled back to the counter to take an order from someone who'd just come in.

"Here's another example," Fred said. "Those pancakes could be raw, and you'd never say a word. You've never complained at a restaurant, and you never will. That's who you are."

Again I considered what he was saying. It occurred to me that if he was right, all I had ahead of me was unhappiness. I called to Bonnie, "Could Manny please put these back on the griddle for another minute or two?"

"He'll make fresh ones," Bonnie said, taking the plate away. "Don't feel bad, Lou. I couldn't eat them that way, either."

ſeventeen

FROM THE STEPLADDER I secured a silver bell to a branch near the top of the tree. Then I climbed down to make sure the ornaments weren't clumped together. Charlotte would have hung the tinsel strand by strand. I did my best to follow her rules: No balls of similar color on the same branch, big ornaments at the bottom of the tree. The collection of crystal ornaments that Sam's parents had added to each year dangled from the ends of the branches where they could best catch the light.

At nine that morning, the nursery had delivered the tree — a balsam because the owner had assured me that its aroma would last longest. It would be a complete surprise for the girls. They had no idea that I'd spent an hour the week before getting the owner to unwrap tree after tree until I found this one, the perfect size and shape.

It was eight days before Christmas. My shopping was almost done. Fred had come up with most of the ideas for the girls. "I'm just a fly on the wall," he'd said when I asked how he knew so well what they wanted. We picked out roller skates and a leather jacket for Annie, and a real telescope for Sara. Now that she was getting bored with the attic, Fred had decided she was ready to discover the heavens. I was giving Fred a cashmere scarf that I'd seen him fondle longingly in the men's department the day he was helping me choose a sweater for Sam.

When I stretched to fasten the angel to the tip of the tree, the ladder trembled and I lost my footing. I tried to catch my balance on the curtain rod, but it slid from its bracket. As I fell, I grabbed at pine needles and drapes. Landing I cried out, then extricated myself from the stepladder and patted my hip. "You'll live," my mother would have said.

"How can you be so sure?" I used to argue when I was little and had fallen. She'd answer me with one of her looks.

She could be sharp at times. She didn't hand out sympathy unless it was absolutely necessary. I'd struggled to figure out what she would like best for Christmas and finally decided on a set of professional kitchen knives. Jack had ordered the set from one of his merchandisers, knives with smooth cherry handles. Now, the only person left on my list was my father, and I didn't see why I should get him anything.

I climbed the ladder again and slid the curtain rod back in place. Then I was done. The tree quivered in expectation, tiny white lights blinking from branch to branch.

But at the last minute I remembered that when the girls were discovering the tree, Charlotte used to play the overture from the *Nutcracker Suite*. As they charged in, I hurried over to the piano and missed seeing the expressions on their faces.

The next thing I knew, Annie had dropped down on the couch and was sobbing. I quickly stopped playing and went over. Sara was standing beside her sister, uncertain what to do.

"What happened?" I said.

Sara gingerly patted Annie. "She's okay."

"She doesn't look okay."

"I'm okay," Annie said, sniffing.

"Tell me what's wrong so I can do something about it."

She shook her head. "You can't."

"Let me at least try."

"It's too late."

"What's too late?"

"It's already done."

"The tree," Sara said to me.

"Wasn't I supposed to do it? Last year when I didn't, you said I should have."

"I liked last year," Annie said, drawing her sleeve across her nose. "I liked doing it."

"Last year every time I put something on the tree, you took it off and put it somewhere else," Sara said. "I didn't like last year."

"You have absolutely no artistic ability whatsoever," Annie said.

"You can do it every single year after this," I promised her.

"I didn't mean to cry," she said to me later, when we were doing the dishes together. "I don't know why I cried."

"It's okay to cry now and then," I told her. "It's okay to show how you feel."

She thought a moment, then said, "Remember when you picked us up at the airport this summer, after we were in California? You hugged Sara but you didn't hug me."

I remembered Annie's shoulders that day, square and sharp beneath her skimpy tank top. "I never know if you want me to," I said.

She sighed. "Do I have to tell you everything?"

On Christmas Eve I drove in to the city with a tin of cookies and a bottle of wine for Mrs. Rapetti. "You didn't give me time to prepare," she grumbled, hanging my coat in the hall closet.

"How's Vinnie?" I asked. I took my sweater off. As usual, the windows of Mrs. Rapetti's apartment were shut tight with the curtains drawn, and the heat, at full blast, filled the room with a cabbagey mist.

"How's Vinnie, how's Vinnie, everyone always asks how's Vinnie, when it's me who's going to be gone someday," she said. "Vinnie's Vinnie. I like to kill him sometimes, but he's all I got." She took two glasses from the dish drainer and poured us each some wine.

"I stopped at the pizzeria to say Merry Christmas," I said. "Vinnie's always smiling."

"You gotta be stupid to smile all the time," Mrs. Rapetti said. "His father used to say, 'Wamme to smack that grin right off your face?' He didn't understand Vinnie." She shook the cookie tin. "What's this?"

"Pfeffernüsse," I said. "Christmas trees. Stars. The girls and I made cookies all day yesterday."

Mrs. Rapetti sighed. "I used to make pignoli cookies at Christmas. I had a beautiful tree — all silver — but the way Vinnie smokes, I got scared it'd go up in flames, so I gave it to my sister-in-law." She twisted off the top of the tin. "You should of called first. I could of made something. I should of bought a piece of green for the door." She stared around the room. "What am I gonna give Vinnie? What am I gonna get for him to give me?"

"We could go out," I said. "There's a men's shop around the corner. We could buy him a tie."

"What would Vinnie do with a tie? He'd hang himself by accident."

"Well, a nice, warm flannel shirt, then."

"He sweats too much for flannel." She nibbled a cookie, then poured each of us more wine.

"A wallet?"

"Some nights," she said. "Some nights I pray to God to take Vinnie. Then I get down on my hands and knees and beg He don't listen to a stupid old woman like me. It's just I get worried, I tell Him. Who's gonna take care of Vinnie when something happens to me?"

She lifted her dress so I could see her legs. "My veins're getting so bad, one day I won't be able to make it down the stairs no more. Vinnie don't know how to take care of nothing. He can't fix himself a cup of coffee."

"You could teach him."

"Coffee grinds everywhere and who's gonna clean up? My husband, he used to say, 'Something happens to me, Carmela, you put the kid in a home.' But then I'd be all alone."

"What was your husband like?" I said.

Mrs. Rapetti narrowed her eyes. "You've seen pictures."

"Dark hair. That's what I remember."

"He was a beautiful man. His hair — he slicked it back,

but underneath it was all curls, like a baby. The night we got married, he said, 'I got nothing else to do in this world but make you happy.'"

"Did he?"

She shrugged. "He was a beautiful talker, too. He could of been a priest. His mother wanted him to be one."

"Was he religious?"

"Tony?" Mrs. Rapetti laughed. "He thought God played him a dirty trick, giving him a son like Vinnie. Once I went to the priest, I said, 'You gotta talk to him, Father.' I was afraid he was going to lose God's grace, the things he was saying. The priest told Tony that Vinnie was one of God's innocents, that he could never sin. Impossible he should ever sin. 'Think about that,' the priest said. But Tony, he said, 'Personally, I like a little sinning in a kid.'" She shook her head. "It was a disappointment to Tony. I should of had another baby. But I was afraid. What if I had another Vinnie?"

"You sure you don't want to go out and get him a present?" I said. "I'll come with you."

"Nah. I don't go out in weather like this. What if I fall? What if something happens to me? What happens to Vinnie then? Who would he turn to? My sister in Jersey? Forget it. I asked her once. She's his godmother, after all. I said, 'Maria, you'd take Vinnie, wouldn't you, if something happened to me?' She said, 'Anything else I'd swear it on the Bible, Carmela. But please, not Vinnie.'"

I reached for my sweater. "Don't go," said Mrs. Rapetti. "Vinnie'll be home soon. I'm making pasta e fagioli."

"I should get back. It's Christmas Eve."

"I didn't buy him nothing. What kind of mother am I?"

The clock on the mantel ticked loudly. "Do you have a piece of paper?" I said.

Mrs. Rapetti looked suspicious. "What for?"

"To write down my number. In case you or Vinnie needs something."

At the door, Mrs. Rapetti took one of my hands and held it to her cheek. Her skin was rough and damp. "Look," she said. "That wine's gone straight to my head." She kissed me good-bye. "You're a good girl," she whispered.

After leaving Mrs. Rapetti, I made myself go upstairs to check on my apartment. I'd spent practically every penny of my savings hanging on to it, but I could hardly bear to step foot inside. Everything in the place meant something to me. An easy chair had come from Aunt Clara's last home before she moved in with my grandfather. "Maybe if you had it re-upholstered," Charlotte used to say each time she saw it, but I liked to think of Aunt Clara sitting down on this very fabric.

"What do you want that piece of junk for?" my mother had said about a standing lamp from when she and my father were first married. It had been up in the attic for more than twenty years, but she still didn't know if she wanted to give it away.

"It's perfect for reading," I'd said to convince her.

"Your place is cluttered enough."

"It'll fit in Richard's trunk. I'll borrow his car and bring it home."

"Richard won't like it."

"He hardly ever comes to my apartment anyway."

"Look at the line on that piece," my mother had said, her hands on her hips. "It's probably a collector's item. I better hang onto it."

It took me years to wheedle that lamp away from her. Now I turned it on to see my other treasures better.

My mother was right. The place was cluttered. Against one of the walls were a table and a desk. The desk was scarred, with a stained leather blotter, but it had been Richard's and its compartments were stuffed with letters from him. The harvest table was a monster, and I opened it only if I was having people for dinner. Charlotte and I had found it upstate and spent several weekends sanding and refinishing it. When it was finally ready, I'd rented a van to bring it home from her garage.

After Vinnie helped me carry it up the four flights, I'd

dropped into a chair and cried. Even folded into its narrowest position, the table was too big, too perfect, for the room. On her next visit, Charlotte had been pleased. "Now you can get rid of some of this junk," she said, but I never did.

On the rim of my bathtub was a carton of congealed bath oil called Essence of Spring, which a student had given me for Christmas a few years back. Holding it up to my nose, I sneezed, and I pictured an earnest scientist stirring a boiling caldron of esters, trying to recreate a garden about to bloom or an April rain. He'd failed; the scent was fake and unconvincing, but it was all I had, and I filled the tub, stripped off my clothes, and slipped in. I lay back, and there was the ceiling, a map of kidney-shaped yellow stains and curlicues of peeling paint which by some miracle never dropped off. It was then, don't ask me why, looking up at that dilapidated ceiling, that I knew I was home.

When I finally reached my mother's house, she was lifting a macaroni and cheese casserole out of the oven. She frowned. "Get me a trivet, quick. Where on earth have you been?"

"Nowhere."

"You were a long time nowhere," she said. "I had to make another trip to the mall. The girls suddenly realized they had presents for everyone but their Aunt Lou."

"They told me they were all done with their shopping," I said.

"If you'd make a list like everyone else, it would be a lot easier for us. No one has any idea what you want. I left the tags on in case you want to return the things I bought you."

I hung my coat behind the door. "Run see who wants what to drink," said my mother.

In the living room, Sara was saying, "So he pretends like he's a woman. He dresses up in women's clothes. But then he meets this beautiful girl and falls madly in love with her."

"What does everyone want to drink?" I asked from the doorway.

"Why, it's Charlotte," Aunt Clara cried.

They all turned to look. "Aunt Clara, it's Lou," Sam said, coming over and putting his arm around me.

"You're slipping," my grandfather said to his sister.

When Aunt Clara still looked puzzled, I tried to think of ways to help her know me. I could tell her that what distinguished me from Charlotte was my right profile. At that angle, it was easy to see the bump on my nose from when Charlotte hit me with a wooden block. But how I most differed from my sister was that I took life as it came. When I was little and my mother's car broke down and she was forty-five minutes late picking me up from the dentist, I waited calmly as the sky darkened. I wasn't afraid she'd forgotten me. I didn't imagine the terrible things that could have happened. I just figured that she had a flat. "Any other child would have been hysterical," my mother said. Every time I heard her tell that story, I'd think, That calm little girl is me.

During dinner Sara asked where Fred was.

"He and his mother have their own tradition on Christmas Eve," I told her. "They have fish soup and open presents."

"We could have something fancy like fish soup if I didn't have to worry about last-minute presents and a big dinner tomorrow," my mother said.

"Now don't start complaining, Liz," Aunt Clara said. "You know you love it."

My mother sighed. "I do and I don't."

"You do and you do," said Aunt Clara. "Charles, what are you so quiet about?"

"I was wakened from my nap by pounding and screams, and I haven't fully recovered yet," said my grandfather.

"How were we supposed to know anyone would be sleeping on Christmas Eve?" Sara asked.

My mother held the serving spoon over the casserole and looked around the table. "Who wants more? Someone must. I don't have room in the fridge for leftovers."

Sam held out his plate.

"So, how is Fred?" Aunt Clara said, looking at me.

"He's celebrating," I said. "He finished the first draft of his book."

"Now, why didn't you tell me?" said my mother. "That's wonderful news."

"When I was in school, I used to think I'd write a book one day," Sam said. "It must really give you a feeling of accomplishment."

"Fred says he feels like throwing his typewriter out the window," said Annie.

"Would it break?" Sara asked. "If it landed in the snow?"

"That's just an expression, saying you're going to throw your typewriter out the window," said my mother. "Fred doesn't have that kind of temper. He's a very even-keel sort of person. Like Lou."

"Aunt Lou?" said Annie.

"I don't see any other Lous around."

"You think Aunt Lou is an even-keel person?"

"Of course she is," my mother said firmly. "Calm. Steady. Reliable. Always in control."

Annie giggled.

"What are you laughing about?" my mother asked.

"Aunt Lou's not like that at all."

"Since when are you such an expert? I've known my daughter her entire life, and I think I know her a little better than you do."

"Look," said Annie, pointing at me.

My mother turned. "What's this?" she said. "Lou? You know you never cry."

After dinner we sat in front of the fire and took turns the way we always did, saying what we wanted most from Santa Claus. Annie went first. She wanted a computer, a VCR, and a leather jacket.

"That's a little greedy, isn't it?" said my mother.

"I've only been asking for a computer two years already," Annie said.

"Maybe Santa Claus doesn't think you should have one," said my mother.

Sam winked at me. He'd finally bought Annie a computer.

When it was my turn, I said, "Come back to me in a minute. I'm not ready. I have to think." I made the same excuse every year.

"Just say whatever comes to mind," my mother urged me. "Earrings, you like earrings. A sweater. It doesn't have to be anything big."

"You could ask for a book," Annie suggested.

"I know what Aunt Lou wants," Sara said.

"What?" I asked.

Sara giggled. "A baby."

For the second time that evening, everybody stared at me. "Well, that's natural," Aunt Clara finally said. "That's a very natural instinct."

"It's your biological clock ticking," said my mother.

"There's only one way to get a baby," Aunt Clara said. "And it ain't Santa Claus."

"That's not true," Sam said. "There's lots of ways to get babies these days. In vitro fertilization, in vivo fertilization, embryo implantation —"

"Wait a second," I said. "Sara said I wanted a baby. Not me."

"Well, don't you?" said Sara.

I'd spent years learning not to want what Charlotte had, fighting envy and desire. I refused to admit that I might want something she already possessed. I never knew if I wanted what I had because I truly wanted it, or because it was something she didn't want. I was a mystery to myself.

"Aunt Clara, it's your turn," my mother said when I didn't answer.

"We all know what this one's going to be," said my grandfather.

Aunt Clara had been wanting the same thing for as long as I could remember, but now she stared blankly at her brother. "Don't tell me."

"You can't have forgotten," he said, frowning.

"Give me a second."

"World peace!" Sara cried.

Aunt Clara smiled. "Of course."

Just then, the doorbell rang. "Who's this going to be?" said my mother, getting up. "Pop, your turn."

"It's probably Fred. He said he might stop by," I said.

But it wasn't Fred.

At the door, my mother gave a little gasp. She took a step backward, and my father stepped forward, as if they were dancing.

His skin was the color of coffee, the same as the leather jacket he had on. His hair, long ago gone gray, was now slick and black. "What have you done to yourself?" my mother said, once she'd caught her breath.

"It was on sale," said my father, proudly dusting the sleeve of the jacket.

"You look ridiculous." He glanced down, flexing his foot in a shiny new loafer. "I mean, you don't look yourself. That's what I mean," my mother said.

"That's it!" My father snapped his fingers. "I'm not myself. I'm a new man."

"Well, I'm the same old woman," said my mother, folding her arms around her middle.

My grandfather stood up. "No, Charles," whispered Aunt Clara, but he'd already moved past her to the door.

"Welcome home, Phillip," he said. He and my father shook hands. "You couldn't have arrived at a more opportune moment. Liz was just about to tell us what she wants for Christmas."

But my mother shook her head. "It's your turn, Pop."

"Now, Elizabeth," he said sternly. "You tell Phillip what it is you want."

She looked at him, biting her lip like a little girl. "Oh, Pop, I don't know."

"You do," he said.

Her lips uncurled. She fiddled with her belt buckle, then brought her fingertips to her forehead, half covering her face. She whispered, "I want my baby back."

eiGHteeN

THE FIRST FEW WEEKS that my father was home, my mother acted standoffish. "Him," she said, instead of "Phillip" or "your father," and when I called to invite the two of them to dinner the day after Aunt Clara and my grandfather went home, my mother said, "I'd love to come, but I can't speak for anyone else."

She continued to work at the restaurant, which meant that my father had to drive her back and forth if he wanted to use the car. He didn't complain, but I started to feel that my mother was going out of her way to get back at him.

"There's nothing going on between you and Jack, is there?" I asked her one day.

"Did your father tell you to find out?"

I shook my head. "Is there?" I repeated.

"Don't be silly. You know I can't stand mustaches."

"Then why do you talk about Jack all the time in front of Dad?"

She sighed. "You've got a lot to learn about men, honey."

Although I hated to admit it, she was right. For instance, the airplane ticket to St. Martin that Fred had given me was still in my possession. Something had to be done. I should never have agreed to think it over that night on Fred's doorstep. If I'd said no firmly and at once, Fred and I might have been able to stay friends. But once I gave him the ticket back after all this time, I knew he was going to stop hanging around.

.   .   .

After a month of freezing weather, the temperature suddenly soared into the fifties, and for a few days, it felt more like spring than like January. When my father came over after lunch one day, his jacket hung open and he wasn't wearing any gloves.

He'd taken to stopping by to see me when my mother was working. Even though we'd never spent much time alone together, it didn't seem at all strange to be sitting down for a chat with him instead of with my mother. There were none of the endless pauses I'd have expected; the two of us could even sit together without saying anything.

"Spring's right around the corner," my father said that afternoon, stamping his shoes on the doormat to get the mud off.

"It's not even Groundhog Day. We could still have a lot of winter left."

"Maybe," he said. "But somehow I just don't think so."

While I made tea, he leaned against the counter, singing, "Oh, do you remember sweet Betsy from Pike, she crossed the wide prairies with her lover Ike." That was a favorite tune of his, along with the one that went, "In Dublin's fair city, where girls are so pretty, I first set my eyes on Sweet Molly Malone." The girls in his songs were sweet, but not the one he'd chosen years ago. On Christmas Eve, after she was done crying, my mother had announced in front of everybody, "I'll take you back, Phil, but don't think this means I forgive you any of your shenanigans."

"Lou," said my father, when we were seated across from each other at the kitchen table and I'd poured the tea. "There's something I have to tell you."

I put my cup down.

"Fred came by to see me last night. He wanted to talk. I fixed him a drink and took him into the den. Do you know what he asked me?"

I shook my head.

"For your hand."

"My hand?"

"He wanted my permission to ask you to marry him."

I stared at the slice of lemon floating on the surface of my tea. "What did you say?"

"I told him it was my understanding that asking a father for his permission had gone the way of icemen and horses-and-buggies." My father looked closely at me. "Do you love him?"

When I shook my head, he seemed relieved. "I didn't think so. Fred doesn't strike me as your type. Or anyone's type, for that matter. You know, when you kids were growing up, I tried to be a bit of a father to Fred. Not that I think I had much of a hand in it, but I think he's turned out just fine. Still, there's something . . . can't quite put my finger on it. He's a good-looking fellow, and he's certainly got enough smarts. Seems he's written a book."

My mind raced ahead. Fred had called that morning and invited me to dinner at his house tomorrow, something he'd never done before.

"More tea?" I asked my father.

He pushed his cup forward. "I'm thinking of buying a moped," he said. "That way your mother could take the car, and we'd both have our freedom."

"You're welcome to use our car, Dad. I mean it. I never go anywhere."

"Well, you should," he said.

"Why a moped?" I asked, not giving him a chance to get started on me. Since he'd come home, he'd been worse than my mother about urging me to go out more, visit friends and so on.

"More economical than a car," he said. "Easier on the legs than a bicycle. Your mother and I rented mopeds on our honeymoon in Bermuda."

"What does Mom say about a moped?"

He grinned. "I think I'll surprise her." He swallowed the last of his tea and stood up. "One more thing. Did you see the paper today?"

"I haven't had a chance to look at it yet."

"Page C-7 might interest you." He doffed his cap. "I'm off."

After he left, I searched around for the newspaper. Sam had left it on the couch, and I opened to C-7, the entertainment page. I saw right away what my father had wanted me to see. Richard's movie was opening at a small theater a few towns away, the only place around where you could see foreign films and documentaries.

I looked up at the clock, and without another thought, wrote a note to Annie and Sara saying not to worry, I'd be home to make dinner. Then I drove like mad to make the two o'clock showing. Since the day of the blizzard, I hadn't heard from Richard. Seeing his movie would give me a reason to call him.

At two in the afternoon, the theater was practically empty. When Richard's name appeared on the screen in strong black print, there was no one I could nudge and whisper to, "I know that guy."

The years that I was with Richard, I'd read drafts of his screenplay, so many that I'd memorized portions of the dialogue. But that didn't prevent a thrill from passing through me as I finally heard those lines spoken. Sitting in that theater, I couldn't help but feel hope. Richard had proven true one of my mother's favorite mottoes, Where there's a will, there's a way.

Midway through the movie, the main character and his girlfriend go off for a weekend at the country home of some friends. When I told Annie I didn't know about a sex scene, I'd been lying. Richard and I had argued over it. Along the way, the guy pulls off a leafy highway, parks the car, and leads his girlfriend into a thicket. Ferns cushion and hide them, and her hair hangs loose. The scene is movement — light and limbs. Only Richard and I knew that it was all wrong. The air that day, I remembered, was muggy, and by the time Richard and I finally got up, my hair was plastered to my forehead and neck.

When I had first read Richard's description of that scene, I'd asked, "Why do movies have to be so phony?"

"So they can get PG ratings," he'd told me.

Arriving at the home of their friends, the guy and his girlfriend mingle with the other guests around a picnic table spread with sandwiches and salads and vases of peonies. Everyone is talking and laughing, until a tall, attractive woman appears in the doorway of the house, wearing a minuscule bikini that wins the attention of everyone but her husband. Busy making certain that all his guests have a cold beer, he hardly notices his wife.

With one eye on her husband, she flirts with the protagonist, teasing him about bringing along yet another new girlfriend and asking him when he is ever going to settle down. Soon, they drift apart from the rest of the group and follow a path through the woods which leads to an enormous shaggy pine tree.

Although that scene had been filmed in northern California, the tree seemed identical to the one on my grandfather's property. I suddenly remembered leaving Charlotte and Richard beneath it and going off for a swim, then waiting by the lake until it would have been embarrassing to be found waiting that long.

In the movie, the woman sulks. "I've had it! He's impossible. You'd think I was invisible." She's lovely to look at, but in the light sifting through the pine needles, her nose is a little too strong, jutting out from the shadow of her face.

"He didn't mean it," says the protagonist. "He didn't see you at first."

She looks away.

"Tell me," he says.

When she turns back to him, her entire demeanor has changed. Her shoulders slump, her eyes are sad. "We've been together so long, he thinks he knows everything there is to know about me. I'm like an old shoe. But he doesn't know everything. He doesn't know that last month, one day when the kids were at school, I threw everything into a suitcase and wrote notes to him and the kids. He doesn't know I took off. He doesn't know that.

"I drove down the block," she continues. "I was never going back. But then, at the corner, an old lady with a cane started crossing the street, and I had to wait and wait, and while I was waiting, I realized I didn't know whether to turn right or left or keep going straight. Where was I headed? I didn't have a clue. By the time that old lady made it to the curb, I'd lost my nerve. I went back and saw the notes I'd written, and then it hit me that the kids would have come home first and they'd have been the ones not to find me there."

She's crying by then. Watching, I could scarcely breathe. The guy pats her shoulder. "It's okay," he says. And when she finally calms down and wipes her eyes, he bends so the branches of the tree brush his head, and he kisses her.

After the movie was over, the lights came on and a woman edged past me, but I didn't move. I couldn't. I had seen a ghost, three times life size. It could have been Charlotte up there on the screen. Somehow, Richard had captured her.

"Ma'am," said an usher in a short scarlet jacket. "I have to clear the theater before the next show."

In the car I tried to sort things out. It seemed impossible that I wouldn't have noticed that Charlotte was unhappy. It crossed my mind that Richard had made the whole thing up. But the actress playing Charlotte had brought goose bumps to my skin, so closely did she resemble my sister. It wasn't that they looked alike; the similarity went deeper than that. The actress carried her sadness the way I imagined Charlotte would have; even in distress, she was sure. One thing was undeniable — Richard had been watching Charlotte as closely as I ever had.

She'd been right not to confide in me. I'd never given her comfort before. Too busy comparing the two of us, I'd never really listened to what she was saying.

I remembered more and more about that day. Charlotte

was suffering from a headache, and I hadn't been very sympathetic. I remembered, too, as if it were yesterday, how everyone had stopped when Charlotte finally made an appearance, how within moments of her arrival we'd flocked to her side, how Annie and Sara were pulling at her arms for attention.

Before I knew it, the turnoff for home was upon me, and I was driving too fast to stop. Braking and pulling onto the shoulder, I jerked the car to a halt.

They say that in the instant before a violent death, a person's entire life flashes before his eyes, but all at once I knew what had crossed Charlotte's mind when the car slipped from her control and she realized that there was nothing she could do. If she screamed — the truck driver had thought he'd heard a sound — she was screaming for the girls. How would they know that she hadn't meant to leave them? How would they know they were her most true loves?

NiNeTeeN

To FRED's HOUSE the next evening, I wore the same jeans and sweater I'd had on all day. I purposely didn't change clothes, didn't even comb my hair or put on lipstick. Fred, to my dismay, was freshly shaven, in a striped shirt and gray flannels, and as he led me into the living room, I caught a whiff of spicy cologne.

On an old brass tray table were bottles of gin and tonic and a plate with quartered limes. While Fred mixed drinks, I sat down, choosing a chair instead of the couch.

"Have you ever been snorkeling?" he asked, handing me a tall glass.

I shook my head.

"I've been reading up on St. Martin. The guidebook says it's a terrific place for snorkeling."

"I don't think I want to go snorkeling," I said. "I don't mind putting my face in the water, but I hate diving."

Fred grinned. "What a relief. I don't want to go, either. I figure I should learn how to swim first."

"You don't know how to swim?"

He shook his head.

"I thought everybody knew how to swim."

"Not me."

"You didn't learn at camp?"

"I went to music camp," he explained. "We just fooled around in the water."

"But you came to the pool with us," I said. "I distinctly remember you having a black inner tube."

"I held onto that tube for dear life."

"But you must have gone off the board," I said.

"Never."

"I'm sorry. I'm surprised, that's all."

"One day, I'll learn," he said. "I've signed up for lessons a few times. Trouble is, the water at the Y is always freezing." He leaned forward, both hands on his knees. "Maybe on vacation you'll teach me."

"Fred," I said. "I'm not going to St. Martin with you."

"We could go somewhere else —" he started to say, but I stood up.

"Not anywhere," I said, looking around for a place to set my untouched drink. "Thank you for asking me, but no."

I should have stopped right there, but for once, the words kept coming. "I'm sorry. I should have told you sooner. I didn't know how to say it. I think the world of you. You've been wonderful to the girls and me. I don't know what we'd have done if you hadn't come around. But you and me — it's not spellbinding. It's not love."

The way I remembered him from childhood, no matter how far the other boys pushed him, no matter how often Charlotte said no, Fred's smile never left him. But when I finally dared to look at him, his smile was gone, and without it, his face was as cold and pale as porcelain.

He got up and walked out of the room. Taking the hint, I followed him down the hall to the foyer.

Although he was only a tiny infant when he and his mother were left alone, Fred had clear memories of his father — cold hands and quiet footsteps. The time he told me that was the time I'd come closest to loving him. Suddenly, I couldn't bear to leave Fred by himself in that lonely, rented house full of things that didn't even belong to him. I wished I felt different. I wished I could marry him. On a winter night, his bulk alone would reassure me. For the wedding, my father would pull out his tuxedo, and my mother, her yellow chiffon, if it still fit. I'd wear my grandmother's dress, and everyone would be smiling, and afterward, my grandfather would place a photograph of me on his mantel. It wasn't that I couldn't imagine the whole thing, just that it seemed more like an ending than a beginning.

Fred opened the front door and stepped aside for me to pass. Before leaving, though, I wanted to touch the C-shaped scar on his chin, a scar he'd received when he was trying to play ice hockey with the other sixth-grade boys. I'd been there. Like everyone else, I laughed when Fred fell, and I ran when I saw the blood.

What happened next happened so fast that only afterward did I figure out exactly how it went. My hand never even grazed Fred's chin. Before I could touch him, he socked me with a strong left hook. Then he disappeared inside, slamming the door, and I was left alone on his front porch.

Minutes must have passed, but I do not recall them. I don't know when I would have moved if Sam hadn't appeared. Out of nowhere, it seemed, there he was, hurrying up the walk.

He tilted my head toward the light. In the cold the bleeding had stopped, but I winced when he touched me. "Poor nose," he said.

"It's okay."

"It looks like he hit you pretty hard."

"I'm fine."

"You're lucky it's not broken." Sam gently felt my cheekbones, then pressed his fingers toward my nose.

"All right, it hurts," I said, pulling away. "I admit it, it hurts."

"I should have driven over," Sam said. "I wasn't thinking. When Fred called, I just grabbed my coat and ran out."

"Fred called you?"

"Let's get you home." Sam wound his scarf around my neck. "I never knew Fred had a temper," he said.

"It was my fault."

Sam patted my shoulder and examined my nose again. "He hit you pretty hard."

We hurried the few blocks home, but when we got there, I said, "I don't want the girls to see."

Sam nodded. "Not your parents either." He thought a moment, then put his arm through mine and pulled me across Nan Gordon's lawn.

He rang her bell three times before she came to the door. "Lou's in trouble," he said.

The two of them led me into Nan's kitchen and sat me down at the counter. Nan unwrapped the scarf and peered into my face. She already had her cold cream on for the night.

"It's starting to bleed again," she said.

"Can you handle this?" Sam asked her. "I should get back."

"Don't worry, I know all about this sort of thing," Nan said. "My brothers were always getting into messes."

"Make up something to tell the girls," I told Sam.

"Of course," he said, resting one hand on my shoulder and the other on Nan's.

After he left, Nan went over to the refrigerator. I stood up, grasping the edge of the counter to steady myself. But coming back with a wad of soggy paper towels and some ice, Nan made me sit down. "Lou, you've got to be still," she said, pushing my hair off my face as gently as she would have touched a seedling.

She sat down beside me and wiped the dried blood away. Then she had me lay my head on her lap. "Does that hurt?" she said, as she stanched the new blood. "It will, no matter what I do."

I must have dozed a little while, my head resting on her lap. The next thing, I was sitting up and she was draping an afghan around my shoulders.

"Everything I say comes out wrong," I said.

Nan smiled. "I'm the same way. That's one of the reasons I dance."

"I always try to think of what Charlotte would say."

"She was never at a loss for words, that's for sure," Nan said. "Not once did I hear her admit she didn't have an answer. She'd always come up with something. She found a way to get rid of Japanese beetles when everyone else in the neighborhood had thrown up their hands."

Hearing Charlotte praised, I was filled with pride; but then, just as inevitably, misgivings kicked in. I'd spent the first part of my life raising Charlotte up on a pedestal, and the next part, trying to knock her off. Faultfinding had become second nature to me. Like a building inspector, I kept an eye out for what would make a structure crumble; then I'd have a reason to condemn it.

"It used to drive me crazy, sometimes," Nan said. "She could be the biggest know-it-all." But then, perfect Madame Gordon was flushed and stammering, "I'm sorry, I don't know why I said that. I'm impossible without her."

All those months I'd controlled my longing for Charlotte, but as I reached for Nan to let her know it was okay, the longing rose in my throat until I could taste it, like a bitter pill not swallowed fast enough.

By the time I got home, the sky was turning light. I went upstairs to check on the girls. They were in their usual sleeping positions, Sara on her back, her hair fanning over the pillow, Annie with her feet sticking out from the covers, because otherwise she felt suffocated.

Their bedspreads were nubby, the carpet worn. The curtains needed to be replaced. In the fall I'd asked the girls if they wanted to redo their room. I brought home wallpaper samples for them to pick from. But both of them said no. The way their room was now, their mother's arm had guided the paintbrush, her fingers had stitched the curtains, and the threadbare carpet and faded floral bedspreads were what she'd chosen.

Annie and Sara were snoring. They claimed they didn't, but I'd heard them often enough through the wall that separated their room from mine. I'd always intended to record the sound of their snores, as proof, but I could never drag myself out of my warm bed to do it.

There was a tape recorder around somewhere. With questions Charlotte thought up, the girls used to interview guests with it. "What was the most embarrassing moment of your entire life? Do you dream in color or in black and white? Do you eat your skin when it peels?"

I went into Charlotte's room and searched her closet, standing on the dressing table stool to reach the top shelf. There, I found the red cable knit sweater I'd been missing for years. I'd suspected that Charlotte had stolen it, but she never stopped denying her guilt.

Not finding the tape recorder, I tiptoed downstairs to check and see if it was in the study. When I passed the couch with Sam asleep on it, I picked up the blanket he'd kicked to the floor and covered him. He was snoring, too.

In the study, I sat down and absently glanced around the desk. A pile of bills beneath a clay octopus paperweight that one of the girls had made in arts and crafts. A clear plastic cube with a photograph on each side. A pencil holder made out of a frozen orange juice can. The Mickey Mouse phone that Charlotte had given Sam on his thirty-fifth birthday.

I picked up the receiver, then replaced it. According to Sam's desk clock, it was only ten past six. I waited a minute or two, then I went ahead and dialed.

The phone rang and rang, and I was beginning to wonder if Richard had gone out of town again, when finally, someone answered. "This better be good," said a woman with a rusty voice.

I hung up. I touched my nose. It had begun to sting again.

My hand trembling, I reached for Sam's picture cube. There we all were, smiling, awkward, faded. From time to time, Charlotte used to update the cube, but she always kept a few old photos, as reminders.

Someday there'd be snapshots of Sam and Nan, Annie and a boyfriend, Sara graduating from high school. There'd be one of me, alone maybe or maybe with someone. The pictures were going to keep changing.

I got up and left the room. Tiptoeing past Sam again, I went to the hall mirror to examine my nose. But before I had a chance to flick on the light for a better look, I saw a figure hunched on the front steps.

He was never going to stop trying. Once Fred Lacey got an idea in his head, that was it. I'd watched him woo Charlotte. Not until she married somebody else did he finally quit sending her love notes on postcards. He hadn't seen Charlotte in years, didn't even know who she was anymore, and still, now and then, one would arrive in her mailbox, a picture of the Tuileries with the message "*Je t'aime.*"

Charlotte and I had always meant to go to Paris together and hang out on the Left Bank the way Simone de Beauvoir did. But Charlotte married Sam and never got there — it wouldn't be the same, bringing a kid — and I ended up going with Richard, who'd said as we were boarding the plane home, "If only they didn't speak French." In Paris, he needed me to interpret. For that, I had Charlotte to thank. Because of her, I'd learned my French. "You have to," she said when we were in high school and I didn't want to practice conjugating irregular verbs any longer. "It's the language of love."

I tiptoed into the kitchen and slipped my jacket on, then carefully opened the back door, leaning against it while turning the knob. Charlotte and I had learned that silent method in high school. That way, our parents couldn't hear, the times we didn't make it home until dawn.

Carefully, I inched my way down the driveway, still gritty with the sand Sam had tossed over the ice after the blizzard. If Fred turned his head an inch, he'd see me. Passing Nan's, I held my breath, but a branch nearby crackled as its icy coating loosened, and Fred shouted, "Lou!"

I ran.

The sound of pounding footsteps filled my head, taking me back to the time the school bully had been after me. All I'd done was cross some line. That was his method — he'd draw a chalk mark where his victim had to go and dare her to cross it.

At assembly, I'd passed a note to Charlotte, explaining the trouble I was in, and after school, she was waiting outside my homeroom. I knew she was going to be there. She always came through in a pinch.

"Hurry up," she said.

I followed her downstairs to the basement, where only the janitor was supposed to go. We sneaked through the boiler room, across the musty cement floor. "Wait," Charlotte said when we reached the door. She cracked it open and poked her head out.

The coast was clear. We moved like Indians across the schoolyard, then along the sidewalk. Not until a block from home did we feel safe. Charlotte held out her palm, and I slapped it, grinning. We thought we'd tricked the bully, but then, roaring like a lion, he sprang out from behind a tree.

We ran for our lives. My heart hammered as I strained to keep up with Charlotte. He was gaining on me. I could hear his rotten breath. He was a big boy, but he moved like the wind.

My stomach was in knots. I turned around. It was a terrible instinct, but I couldn't help it. I had to see.

When I stumbled, Charlotte grabbed hold of my wrist and kept me from falling. Fingers grazed the flying edge of my jacket, but she wasn't going to let him get me. She wasn't going to let anyone get me — not then, not now. "Lou, don't look back," I heard her gasp that clear winter morning, and I surged forward, out of his reach.